THE VAMPIRE'S CHRISTMAS

MORETTI BLOOD BROTHERS

BOOK FIVE

By Juliette N. Banks

COPYRIGHT

Copyright © 2021 by Juliette N. Banks. All rights reserved.

No part of this book may be reproduced in any form or by any means, electronic or mechanical, including photocopying, recording, or by any information storage and retrieval system without the written permission of the author, except for the use of brief quotations in a review.

This book is a work of fiction and imagination. Names, characters, places, and incidents are either products of the author's imagination or are used fictitiously. Any resemblance to actual persons, living or dead, events, or locales is entirely one of coincidence. The author acknowledges the trademarked status and trademark owners of various products and music referenced in this work of fiction, which have been used without permission. The publication and/or use of these trademarks is not authorized, associated with, or sponsored by the trademark owners.

Author: Juliette N. Banks
Editor: Happily Ever Proofreading LLC
Cover design by: Sheri-Lynn Marean of SLM Creations

ABOUT THE AUTHOR

Juliette is an indie paranormal romance author who has taken the genre by storm with her popular vampire series The Moretti Blood Brothers. She launched her first book in January 2021, and now has seven steamy novels across two series, which readers read faster than she can write.

Juliette has a vast background in consumer marketing and has previously published with Random House. She lives in Auckland, New Zealand, with Tilly, her Maine coon kitty, and all her book boyfriends.

Official Juliette N. Banks website:
www.juliettebanks.com

Instagram:
https://www.instagram.com/juliettebanksauthor

Facebook:
https://www.facebook.com/juliettenbanks
https://www.facebook.com/groups/authorjuliettebanksreaders

DEDICATION

To all the amazing authors who paved the way 'years ago' and achieved independent success. You inspire me every day. Thank you to those who reached out their hand and shared their wisdom and time.

I am forever grateful.

Juliette x

ALSO BY JULIETTE N. BANKS

The Moretti Blood Brothers
The Vampire King (FREE)
The Vampire Prince
The Vampire Protector
The Vampire Spy
The Vampire's Christmas
The Vampire Assassin

Realm of the Immortals
The Archangels Battle
The Archangel's Heart

THE
VAMPIRE'S
CHRISTMAS

CHAPTER ONE

Present Time

Vincent Moretti leaned against the edge of the window and stared across the castle grounds. It looked like it could snow, but it rarely snowed in Rome. And certainly not in early December.
December.
It was the topic of discussion going on behind him which he was trying to ignore, because for fuck's sakes, vampires weren't religious and most certainly did not celebrate their traditions, except his brother had gone and mated a damn human, so guess who wanted a fucking Christmas tree?
And not just a tree.
If Willow Moretti had her way, the whole castle would look like goddamn Macy's in December.
And November.
And October.1
Not that he shopped at Macy's.

"I think it's a lovely idea," Kate said.

Groan.

"Especially with baby Moretti due in the coming weeks," she continued.

Vincent turned to glance at his mate. God, she was gorgeous. On any given day, she was as graceful as all the queens he'd met in his long, eternal life, but she wasn't just *any* queen.

She was his.

Vincent had met Kate just before he'd inherited the Moretti throne. Now she sat on one of the red sofas with a belly so round and full she could be Santa Claus.

Not that he would say that out loud; he'd be eaten alive by any number—if not all—of the new females in their family. An extended family. Once upon a time, it had just been his parents, Brayden, and him. Then just the two of them. Now, he had Kate, Brayden had mated Willow, and her Best Friend Forever—or some shit like that—Brianna had mated Craig, the commander of the Royal Army.

Craig was an extension of their family, and one of the biggest males in the race. While Brianna was a tiny little thing, Vincent had soon figured out if the fiery redhead could handle Craig, she was going to have no problem saying a thing or two when she felt there was any injustice at hand.

Even if it meant confronting the king.

Which he totally respected, though would never let on. As king, you had to be a powerful leader. Always. Still, he was never tested more than when these three females got together and decided they wanted something.

Like Christmas.

"Yes! Then we can buy each other gifts and put them

under the tree to open on Christmas Day," Brianna said, cheering Willow on. "It's the one human tradition I was sad to lose."

Losing their humanity was a recent occurrence for both new females. Willow had mated with Brayden eight months ago and had fortunately chosen to turn into a vampire. If she hadn't, who knows what would have happened. Brayden was the most powerful alpha in the race, and going rogue after being rejected by his mate would have been devastating for them all.

Yet, he'd given Willow the choice.

And they all knew why.

Their father, Frances Moretti, had turned their mother before telling her what he was. When Guiliana Moretti had finally forgiven him, Frances had promised her they would depart this world after a thousand years.

It got worse.

They had asked the two princes to take their heads off on the fated anniversary.

It wasn't Vincent's favorite day of his life.

But Vincent had one fond memory from that fated day. After they'd watched their parents' bodies float away under the rising sun, he'd retired to his quarters. Kate had knocked on his door. Even back then, when he'd had no idea she was his mate, Kate had been the one he needed. They had talked for hours, and she had calmed him.

Now, one hundred and thirty years into his reign and despite her allegiance with these cunning former human females, Kate was the only one he could let his guard down around. His mate. It's true he was extremely close with his brother, but even around Brayden he was still a king and leader. With Kate, he could just be a male.

"See? It's a great idea," Willow announced. "I'll order

the decorations."

Vincent groaned and ran a hand across his chin.

He heard his father's words in his ears: *Pick your battles, son.*

Vincent looked over at Brayden, who was sitting on the arm of a chair rubbing an invisible stain off his pants. His eyes darted to the other side of the room where Craig leaned against a pillar and appeared to be having a manicure emergency by the way he was focusing on his fingernails.

Pussies.

So it was up to him, then.

Vincent walked over and poked at the roaring fire as the three females continued making plans to turn his castle into a winter fucking wonderland.

"Vincent. What do you think, darling?" Kate asked.

I think I'd rather poke my eyes out than wander the halls of my castle draped in stupid glittery balls.

"Compulsory mistletoe on all the doorways," Brianna cheered.

Craig looked up. "No," he growled.

All three females rolled their eyes.

"No one is going to try to kiss me, babe. They all know they'd lose a limb."

Craig smirked. "Good."

Vincent laughed.

"Bray?" Willow asked.

The prince crossed his arms and narrowed his eyes.

Vincent didn't envy the guy.

While all three of their mates were strong-minded, Willow was the most dominant and demanding. And it was because of that the two had mated. No wallflower could mate with such a powerful male.

"It's Vincent's decision," Brayden said. "If he approves it, then the decorations cannot interfere with security, so you'll need to work with one of Craig's guys."

Vincent wasn't surprised his brother had deferred to him. It was why they were such an effective team; Brayden had no desire to be king and respected his authority. Or in this instance, needed someone to pass the buck.

"No, totally. We can do that, right, Bri?" Willow asked.

"Oh, for sure. We'll just need to get those smaller reindeer family displays for outside. You know the one, Willow, with—"

Wait, what?

"Wait a fucking minute!" Vincent finally snapped. "*If* I approve this, and I'm not saying I will, there will be boundaries *on top of* the security rules Bray has rightly mentioned."

When everyone just stared at him like he was that fucking Scrooge duck guy, he lifted a finger into the air. "One," he began, not giving a shit about their pouty faces. "This isn't Disney-fucking-land. If you want to put a decorated tree in the foyer or in one of our family living areas, that's fine. Do gifts or whatever. But I'm not having this placed decked out like an amusement park."

Craig nodded his agreement.

Brianna opened her mouth, thought about it, then closed her lips.

Willow...not so much.

"I mean, that would look naff."

Vincent's eyes narrowed. "Naff?"

"Yeah, like some random tree shoved in a room. There needs to be a theme," she stated.

"Not really," Vincent replied, lifting a brow.

The two of them began a stare off.

"Okay," Brayden interrupted. He was fast becoming an expert in breaking up debates between Willow and him. "Let's see what the females propose and then we can review it. How about that?"

By the look of all the fish mouthing and eye darting, Vincent figured the females weren't on board with his idea.

"Christmas is now," Brianna restated, pointing out the obvious. As if they couldn't tell by her seasonal sweater. Vincent would put money on Craig not complaining about the tight, short, red number, even if it had weird Santa hat patterns on it.

"We need to get decorating *now*," she complained.

"I'm sure we'll all survive without tinsel," Vincent said, rolling his eyes.

"Alright!" Kate spoke firmly, attempting to stand up abruptly and losing her balance. She was weeks away from her due date and moving around was difficult. All of them rushed to assist, but Willow reached her first.

Kate pointed a finger at him. "You. Don't be rude. We're celebrating the holidays for the girls. End of story. We will decorate, but ladies, please ensure security is not compromised."

He would never admit it to anyone, but Vincent loved it when Kate got all queenly.

Fuck, it was sexy.

His eyes burned, and he adjusted his pants as she walked toward him.

"Now, if everyone doesn't mind, I am going to lie down." Kate planted a kiss on his lips, and he grinned. "Play nice," she whispered.

He grinned wider.

"I'll be in to see you later," Vincent said, his hand on her hip and wishing there was no one in the room so he could lift her dress, spread her legs, and hear her scream his name.

Again.

Earlier in the day, he'd had her legs wrapped around his head while he pleasured them both. Pregnancy, it turned out, was quite the aphrodisiac.

"So no reindeer?" he heard Brianna ask as his eyes followed Kate as she walked out of the room. From behind, her long blonde hair flowed down her back in waves. Aside from the way she now walked, you could hardly tell she was pregnant; that is, until she turned, then there was no guessing.

The castle was abuzz with baby talk and staff taking bets on whether it would be a boy or a girl. A new prince or princess being born was a big deal. Despite Willow becoming a princess when she mated Brayden, there had never been a pureblood Moretti princess in history.

Vincent was excited, but recently, he'd been having private freak-outs about becoming a father. Frances Moretti had been an incredible father to him and the prince, so he had no reason to question his ability, but it was still a big deal. He may be a king, but he wasn't a perfect male.

The world they were bringing their child into was a changed one. Now, humans knew about them. Or they had, until they'd taken a page from the human playbook and spun PR like a pro, influencing the masses on social media—aka manipulating them—to believe the breaking news was fake news.

It had worked well so far.

However, the proof provided to the US president,

where the leak had happened, had been enough to force Vincent to face the situation head-on and speak with President Adler. Together, along with dozens of world leaders or their representatives, they had formed a top-secret global operation called *Operation Daylight*. It provided a confidential space for them to share information about their race with high-level officials so they could eventually integrate the knowledge of their existence into the human psyche without everyone losing the damn plot, or in other words, freaking the fuck out and creating a war between the two races.

No one wanted that. Not the Moretti royal family nor the world leaders.

So yeah, Vincent had a few things on his plate; become a father, keep his race safe, and decide what to do with the rebels in the Moretti prison—especially the leader, Stefano Russo—the latter of which, he'd decided, could wait until after the baby was born. That asshole wasn't going anywhere.

So if these females wanted a few Christmas trees, they could have them. Maybe this was the reprieve he was looking for. Something about taking lives, even of those who had wronged him and their race, didn't feel right when they were bringing a new life into the world.

Vincent would do what was needed. But not in the same breath.

He wanted to separate the two things as far as he damn well could. Shedding blood when his son or daughter was about to be born seemed...revolting.

So, it looked like the Morettis were having their first Vampire Christmas.

"Oh, there will be reindeer," Willow replied, nodding.

Like fuck.

CHAPTER TWO

Present Time

Water flowed through her hair as Kate rinsed out her shampoo. She squeezed her hair and poured the lightly scented conditioner into her hand before she began to finger it through her long locks. Next, she clipped it on top of her head and reached for the sponge to wash her body.

"Let me," Vincent said as he slipped into the spacious shower behind her.

He pulled her body up against his as he took the white sponge from her hand. His mouth ran down her neck as she rubbed against his hard erection.

"I don't have long." Kate smiled.

"I'm just here to help you wash," he replied, and she could hear the grin in his voice. "Pour the wash for me."

She tipped the vanilla body wash into the sponge, and he got to work soaping her up.

"Arm up," he ordered, and she tried to hide her smile

as he worked his way over her breasts and around.

"This is my favorite chore of the day." His voice was dry at her neck. "Legs wide."

Kate tried not to gasp as his fingers took over the job of the sponge, slipping in and over her flesh. Teasingly, they moved down her thigh and up over her hip before returning again.

Her head tipped back as his other hand moved over her breast and tugged on her stiff nipple.

"Vincent…" she said, pushing into his cock.

She knew his triggers, and she wasn't above using all of them. Pregnancy had made her super sensitive and horny.

"God, you are sopping wet for me." He groaned.

"Yes. Get inside me now."

Next thing she knew, he had lifted her and vamp sped them to their bed. Vincent sat down and pushed her legs wide.

"Let me clean this up for you," he whispered, gripping her hips and face-planting into her pussy.

Kate cried out, clenching his hair in her hands. "Fuck!"

"Sweet nectar of the fucking gods," Vincent said, his teeth nipping at her clit. "Sit on my cock."

He sat on the bed and pulled her on top of his large body, his strength able to easily lift her additional pregnancy weight and control the speed in which she took him into her body. He was thick and wide, just as she loved him.

When she was fully impaled, he smiled at her and cupped the side of her face.

"Never gets old." He grinned.

"Never," she agreed, laughing and gasping at once.

"Grip my cock," he ordered as they both began to move her along his length. "Yes, God, yes. That's it. Ride me. *Fuck*."

Up and down she moved, clenching him as the heat within her began to build like an inferno. Her whole body buzzed with the need for release. Kate's hands flew to her breasts, and she flicked her nipples.

"So fucking sexy," Vincent growled, speeding her up.

"Touch my pussy," she begged him.

His thumb slipped onto her clit and rubbed in circles, sending her flying.

Her body arched. Her nails dug into Vincent's arms. "Oh God, yes. Yes, yes, yes!"

"That's it, God, yes, Kate," Vincent cried, his arms flexing as he moved her even faster now, milking him.

She felt his cock swell and fill her even more, pushing them both over the edge.

Throwing her head back, she cried out her ecstasy.

Vincent fell back on the bed, and she began to follow him, but his big strong arms reached up to slow her.

"Careful, sweetheart."

She smiled as she glanced down at her swollen belly.

He sat back up and pressed his mouth to hers.

"Fuck, I love you," Vincent declared. "Every minute of every goddamn day."

"I know," Kate replied, smiling as he deepened their kiss. Because she did know, and she had earned his love.

Ten minutes later, Kate slipped her feet into a pair of Prada sheepskin slipper boots and ran her hand over her swollen belly. The midi wool dress she wore in a matching cream color fit snug on her body. It was very different from her usual elegant wardrobe, but when you were eight months pregnant, one didn't give a flying…frog.

She was trying to stop cursing for when the baby arrived, but five minutes spent with the males in the household—especially her mate—gave her little hope that her bundle of joy wouldn't be saying motherfucker before mom.

Kate pulled on the matching full-length cardigan and waddled out of the royal suite. Because yes, one waddled when she was pregnant with the child of such a large vampire. God help Brianna if she ever got with child.

Kate grimaced before laughing to herself.

Stepping out of the royal suite, she took their private elevator down to the first floor and walked toward the rehabilitation center.

Very few people in the castle had access to the new restricted area, and for good reason. Within its walls were the vampires who had survived the unthinkable: being kidnapped by humans using technology developed with the help of Stefano Russo, vampire enemy *numero uno*. A vampire who was thankfully locked in their castle's prison.

Thank God.

Kate felt safer knowing her baby was being born into a world where *soon* he would no longer exist.

Stefano was a dangerous vampire. As leader of the rebellion, he was responsible for so much suffering and deaths, and now torture. The captured vampires had been subjected to scientific testing they didn't fully understand yet. They had suffered indescribable pain over several weeks, unable to move, speak, or help themselves.

Sofia Ferrero—now De Luca—mate to one of their best warriors, Lance De Luca, had discovered them while undercover as their spy. Once a member of the rebellion, Sofia had been arrested and imprisoned in the Moretti castle, but when Lance had discovered she'd been sexually abused by the rebel leader, they'd separated her from the other male prisoners.

During interrogation, they had learned she may be of use to them, and after pledging her allegiance to Vincent, she had returned to the rebellion and more than proved her loyalty. Vincent had recognized in Sofia an ability for great empathy and had invited her to work with the survivors and help with their rehabilitation.

Kate had been pleased. While she adored Willow and Brianna, it was nice having another Italian female in their inner circle; one who had lived during the Victorian period, just as she had, although Kate was much older.

Kate herself was leading the rehabilitation team, working alongside Sofia and the other members for a couple of months, and they were starting to see some progress now.

She walked into the highly guarded entrance and took a breath. Inside, it was different from the castle. The team had erected plaster walls and a ceiling to create what looked like any other office building. It was tranquil with white walls, soft furnishings, and calm lighting. There were a lot of book nooks, sofas with throw blankets, board games, and cards. In one room, they had a gymnasium, and in another, there was a TV room. There were bedrooms and offices down a hall.

"Your Majesty." Sofia smiled as Kate took her place at the head of the table in their meeting room.

"Please, I've told you many times to call me Kate while we're here." She tsked.

Kate took her role as queen very seriously, but there was something about this space that felt sacred. As vampires, it had been a lifelong fear that humans would discover them and turn them into lab rats to learn more about their strengths and abilities, and that's exactly what had happened.

Over the past few months, they'd built bonds, strong bonds, with each other as a management team and the twelve survivors. Their jobs were all about listening and guiding them to a healing place, and that meant listening to their stories, to their silences, and holding a safe space for their tears to flow. It wasn't easy work, but it was important. Their suffering had been so vile it was hard to comprehend. While they were free physically, it was the mind that kept them trapped. Kate and the team strove every day to help them free themselves of that repetitive torment.

Then there were those who had not survived.

The US president, James Adler, had sent a team to the US Army base in Italy where the vampires had been kept in a private and secure lab. He had been shocked and disgusted it was happening on US property, and more than happy to help. The vampires had been flown back to Rome and sped to the Moretti castle. The memories of the US soldiers had been wiped and replaced with some random operation so they no longer remembered vampires existed. This was their life. Always hiding and covering things up. They'd lived like this for thousands of years among humans.

And it was worth it.

If they could turn back time and remain unknown, she knew every single one of them would.

There had been no greater reminder of what could happen if, and when, more humans knew about their race than when the thirty-seven vampires had been recovered, and only twelve of them had survived. They still did not know why. They should have healed.

It had been devastating for everyone.

It had been Willow who'd recommended they be honored.

Vincent had ordered the twenty-five names engraved on a wall inside the Moretti castle and their families invited to a vigil where they told stories of their loved ones until the sun began to rise and their bodies were cast out into the daylight, returning to ash. The king had embraced every single one of them, heavy with guilt for failing to protect those he deemed his.

And they were.

Every vampire was a part of Vincent Moretti. It wasn't a cliché—their life energy ran through his veins, something only a Moretti knew.

"After the king glared at me that time, I just can't," Sofia said.

Kate waved her hand around. "Oh, stop. He glares and growls at everyone."

Sofia laughed.

Three other female vampires and two males stepped into the room, curtsying and taking a seat around the table.

Once a week, they met to go through their guests' charts. They purposely didn't call them patients; this wasn't a hospital, and they all felt it was important to see them as survivors, not victims. Though some days, that was damn hard.

"Good evening, everyone. Let's get started," Kate said. "As you know and definitely can see, I am weeks away from bringing the heir to the throne into the world. When I do, I'll be a little busy." She let the mothers around the table snigger. "Sofia, I want you to lead the team in my absence."

The female's eyes bulged in surprise.

Kate had been looking forward to sharing this with her. While Sofia had been on the wrong side—the rebellion—once, the intelligent and competent female had years of training and experience in leadership. Plus, she was compassionate, caring, and had proven herself to be a great team leader.

There was no doubt in Kate's mind Sofia was the right person for the job. In fact, Kate was planning to be a very hands-on mother, despite having a nanny, and had no plans to step back into the rehabilitation center's leadership role.

She hoped, as they all did, their guests wouldn't need to be here forever. Their goal was to help them heal to the point they could return to a somewhat normal functioning life.

"Oh, *grazie*," Sofia said, thanking her. "This is a great honor."

Kate smiled, nodded gently, and turned to one of the males.

"Wonderful. Let's get started, then. Trent, kick us off."

They each had two guests they were responsible for supporting, and these weekly meetings were an opportunity for them to update her on how things were progressing and to raise any issues. She listened as each of them shared their updates, and was delighted to hear two of their guests were going home this week. The remaining ten still had a little ways to go.

"This is great news. The king and I are committed to this project, for want of a better word, for as long as it takes. I know you aren't, but never pressure any of them," she reminded, looking from face to face with a small smile. "If it takes one year or ten years, that's okay. This is about what's best for each guest."

They all nodded and returned her smile.

Sofia went last.

"Tyler is doing well. He's considering a home visit next week but hasn't made any plans. Yet. As you said, I'm not going to push. He'll do it when he's ready. But my feeling is, it will be soon," she said, looking down at her tablet. "What else? Oh, yes, his shaking hasn't returned, so we think his nervous system has healed."

That was fantastic news.

While vampires healed rapidly, one of the side effects all the survivors had was a chronic shaking. There was no such thing as a "vampire doctor" because they had no need for them; however, many in their race trained and practiced as human doctors. They had reached out to Dr. Abbott, whom they'd connected with in Los Angeles earlier in the year when Vincent had been poisoned, another gift from the psychopath Stefano Russo.

Unfortunately, Dr. Abbott hadn't been able to give them a solid answer during their video call, but he believed the drugs used, combined with the stress they'd endured over the weeks, had slowed down their healing abilities. Like with humans, he'd recommended they simply observe the guests; he would expect, once the substance left their system, they should heal.

It appeared he had been right.

But it had taken months for many of them.

While they were a different species, the spiritual, mental, and emotional impact of abuse was the same as with humans, and Kate suspected, all living beings. There was no quick fix. It simply took time, and everyone had their own internal clock.

Patience and kindness were two virtues they were all practicing.

"That's good news, Sofia. Please update Dr. Abbott; he will be interested. I'd like him to stay appraised of the work we are doing, so please ensure you connect with him often when you step into my shoes," Kate indicated, and Sofia nodded.

"And Anna?"

Sofia tapped her pen on her lips as she stared at her tablet.

"Well...she's still the same." Sofia frowned as she looked up.

They all frowned with her.

"Every day she tells me she's doing fine and busies herself with trying to help the others. She's not facing what happened to her, and, well, you all know how long it's been. I know we just spoke about being patient, but what Anna is doing is avoidance."

In other words, Anna was in denial.

They'd discussed Anna a few times over the past few weeks. She was a young vampire and had a full life ahead of her. At eighty years old, a vampire was considered a teenager; not in the same innocent way a human was but as someone far too young to let the youthful glint in such a vibrant female's eyes die. And it was a mere ember right now.

"Has she left the center?" Kate asked.

The guests weren't treated as prisoners; they would never do that. When they had physically recovered, many had ventured out for drives, walks on the grounds, or even a wander around the castle.

"No." Sofia shook her head.

"Okay, let's start with getting her out and about the castle. See if that triggers anything," Kate said. "She's in a cocoon here, and it's not helping her."

The team murmured their agreement.

"You're right. I'll nudge her," Sofia spoke. "In my experience, it will be something small that breaks her open. A person, a food, or even a smell."

Kate listened as the team continued discussing ideas to help Anna. She mindlessly caressed her belly thinking about how she would give her life to ensure her child was loved and protected, just as she herself had been all her life. Kate had been blessed with lovely parents and a great life up until the day she'd lost them.

While some saw her role as queen as something she'd slipped into with ease, it hadn't been like that. It most definitely hadn't been your roses-and-rainbows romantic novel, that's for sure.

It had been a role she had fought for.

Until the day she'd given up…

CHAPTER THREE

England, 1891

"I'm not going to bow to you, you know that, right?" Brayden asked, leaning against the fireplace which was finally starting to emit some warmth.

England in the winter was dreary and cold, even for a vampire.

Vincent smirked. "You will, or I will take your head."

"Yeah, yeah. You've been threatening to do that all my life." He laughed.

"Ah, but brother, now I can." Vincent grinned, dropping his big body into the armchair.

The prince did the same and put his feet up on the coffee table. If their mother had been alive, he would have been smacked by now.

As if reading his mind, Brayden glanced over and dropped his boots to the floor.

"I miss them."

"Me too," Vincent admitted. "I wish I could ask Father more questions."

"You had hundreds of years. Wasn't that enough time?" Brayden asked, raising an eyebrow.

The answer was no.

"Learning to be a king and *being* a king are two different things," he said. "Haven't you been hearing the whispers and court gossip? They say I don't have what it takes. That I'm a weak king."

Brayden's eyebrows furrowed.

His brother was fearlessly loyal. Obviously, he hadn't heard anything, which in hindsight, was no great surprise. No one would be stupid enough to say such a thing to the alpha prince.

"Weak? Are you fucking kidding me?" Brayden cursed, proving Vincent's mental point. "Do we need to kick some ass? Because I'm up for kicking ass if you are."

Vincent shook his head.

"That's not exactly how it works, brother. I would need to be the one doing the kicking to prove my strength." He let out a dry laugh. "But that's not what's going on here. Underneath their gossip is fear. They're worried I won't, or can't, protect them. Which means I am not doing my job well enough."

"Rubbish!" Brayden, the ever loyal, replied.

Vincent ran his hands over his face.

"Come in!" he yelled when there was a knock at the door.

"Your Majesty." Regan bowed. "I have the pamphlets for your approval."

Regan had worked for his father for centuries as his trusted advisor, and while Vincent had trained alongside his father, he'd built a strong relationship of his own with the vampire. Recently, they'd discussed the growing unease among the race. In truth, his father had foreseen this, as a change of monarch always caused those in resistance to rear their heads. It happened within the human race too.

Regardless, Vincent felt like a failure for not having countered it already.

That he'd been grieving the death of his mother and father and coming to terms with his sudden, although expected, new role was of no interest to the everyday vampire. And nor should it be. They deserved a strong and competent leader. Being born into the role meant he could sit on the throne and wear the crown, but it didn't mean he'd earned it. Now he had to prove himself to his race. He just didn't know how.

That wasn't to say he didn't have some ideas.

Vincent was a strategist more than a warrior, with a fast, quick mind. He would use those skills to influence his vampires and show he had plans to take them into the future and protect them. Humans were showing the days of battle were behind them, and now strength lay in the mind of people like scientists.

Regan had recommended the flyers which would be distributed to vampire households around Europe, where the majority of their race lived. It introduced him as king and shared some of his visions for their future. Even more importantly, it reassured them that he would uphold the values and promise of protection that his father, and his father before him, had given to their race for thousands of years.

Vampires lived a long time, and they had survived by evolving. They would expect him to continue moving their race forward, living in the world of humans while remaining invisible. Because he was their king, and that was his job.

He leaned forward, reviewing the wording, before handing it back.

"This is excellent work. Thank you."

"Thank you, sire. We shall get them printed and begin distribution," Regan said, turning to leave, but then he halted. "I understand there is a growing number of vampires in the new America. Shall we venture further?"

Vincent nodded.

Yes, he'd been aware there were more and more of his vampires emigrating, a fact he found interesting. Many humans and vampires across Europe believed the new continent was the answer to all their financial woes and a source of new opportunities.

He was curious.

The Morettis were always interested in ways to continue investing and growing their fortune. The Manhattan arrival port had been nicknamed the *Golden* Door, and it was becoming so popular they were building a new entry point on Ellis Island to process people.

A seed, which had been planted previously, began to sprout in his mind.

"These are good, Vincent," Brayden said, waving the pamphlet in front of him. "See? You are already doing king stuff. I'm sure these are all normal teething problems. Hell, if we need to, we can go talk to old Queen Victoria and then wipe her mind. I'm sure she has a few stories to tell."

Vincent cringed. "No, thanks."

They might be vampires, but as a wealthy and influential family, the Morettis often attended many of the same events as the Italian and English royals. Queen Victoria was a terrifying woman, even for a strong male like himself.

No one in this household had any interest in a tea party with Her Majesty.

In any case, humans were not vampires. Though he couldn't argue that the psychology between the two species was similar, they had to remember, at the heart of it, vampires were predators, and they wanted to see leadership and strength from him.

It was just going to look different from the strength his father had shown.

Vincent was a physically strong vampire, but he had different ideas about how he would lead. Ideas which would see their species thrive in the evolving modern world. They needed a different kind of leader as they moved forward, and he needed time to showcase his skills. Taking off someone's head to prove himself was not the kind of king he wanted to be.

Or who he was.

If that was what they wanted, they were going to be disappointed.

Vincent needed to be seen circulating with the right people in society, their investments thriving, and moving the race forward. So, if he was stepping into society as the new king, he needed a queen. Not that humans knew he was a king, but the Morettis were seen as a prominent family, and he was now head of said family, which meant adhering to the rules of the time.

He couldn't be seen with multiple women. Behind closed doors and as a vampire, he could be as promiscuous as he liked, but in England, it would be appropriate for him to take a wife. Or in his case, a queen. His mate.

Vincent shook his head as one female came to mind.

Kate.

The memory of her eyes, which had met his during his coronation, still now had his heart beating faster. It wasn't the only part of his body which reacted when she was near.

Vincent knew he'd been hot and cold with her these past several weeks, and yet, when he saw her in passing or at a meal, she remained as polite as always.

Which makes me feel like an ass.

They'd share a few words, a simple glance, and every single time she blushed, his cock would harden. It would be simple for him to rectify the sexual tension between them. He could have her escorted to his chamber and lay her out on his bed, pleasuring her for hours. God, how he wanted to do that.

He had little doubt Kate would desire it, too.

Vincent cringed.

Just the thought of treating her like any other female who flitted through the revolving door of females wanting to bed him or his brother made him mad. For as long as he'd been stroking his cock, females had wanted to assist him to get one step closer to the throne. It was the same for Brayden, yet the difference was that he would never be king.

Vincent was now on the throne. Things were different.

There just were some females who were not made to be enjoyed in the way he and his brother had with some of them. True, it was enjoyment for both parties, and they never harmed any of them, and he never would. He was a Moretti. Every single living vampire was a part of him, and his purpose for being. As king, it was his job to protect them all.

But it was more than that.

Kate was...

He didn't know.

He just knew he could never enjoy her body, take pleasure from her, then see her out the door. He just wouldn't do it.

She was a female who deserved to be adored. Cherished. Fucked so hard she would never consider another male.

The female he did those things with would be his mate. There was no way he could do that with Kate and mislead her. His mate would arrive one day. Mother Nature was in charge of that.

When he found her, he would know.

Brayden finished his whisky and stood. "You know what you need, brother? A good romp. Join us today. Or at least relieve yourself watching if you don't want to partake."

The prince was referring to the endless orgies he hosted nearly every week. He hadn't joined them for a long while, and had recently bitten Kate's head off when he believed she'd attended one.

The thought that she might be there tonight had him jumping to his feet.

"I shall."

Vincent suspected he'd simply walk through looking for her long blonde locks, but his eager pace as he kept up with his brother was well received.

"*Bravo.* I'm pleased to see you so excited to use that heavy thing between your legs." Brayden grinned as he pushed the doors open.

The air changed as they stepped inside the large ethereal space. The air was thick with smoke and lust. Time slowed down to a seductive purr as the bodies around him lay draped over furniture, writhing and arching in pleasure. It felt lazy and delicious.

And yet, Vincent had no interest in participating.

His cock, however, felt differently and stiffened inside his pants. He reached down and adjusted himself.

Brayden slapped him on the back before walking off.

Vincent watched his brother reach up and pull his shirt free, then drop his pants. Around him, vampires salivated at a chance to enjoy the prince. A female crawled over, away from another body, when Brayden wiggled his finger at her. She stopped at his feet, and the prince directed his cock into her willing mouth. Her eyes glittered as she watched Brayden drop his head back, sighing happily. Then he turned and winked at Vincent with a smug grin.

Vincent shook his head.

He'd seen his brother get off more times than he could count. He had no interest in standing around watching.

Across the way he spotted Craig, the commander of his army. The guy was sitting with his legs spread, arms draped over two females who were taking turns on his cock like it was a damn lollipop. He was fingering them, and the wonky grin on his dangerous-looking face showed he had not a worry in the world.

Vincent stepped further into the room, his hand slowly rubbing up and down his shaft. While he was here looking for those damn blonde locks, he was unable to ignore the arousal growing within him. Everywhere he looked, there were thick cocks, swinging tits, and luscious round buttocks in the air.

Not one body in this room would say no to him shoving his cock in any of their orifices—except his brother, and thank fuck for that.

Vincent wasn't a vampire who got high on power. Hell, he had more power than most creatures on . He was the fucking king of a race of predators. Yet he had no desire to take advantage of his position. His mother had told him she'd seen within him strong values which would serve him well as king.

She had been right.

But he didn't want to think about his mother right now; not in the middle of an orgy. And those values did nothing to change the fact he was fucking turned on right now.

Jesus fuck.

He couldn't abstain now that he was king. It could take him one hundred years to meet his mate, or longer. He'd eventually have to find the type of female to find relief with, wouldn't he? Wanking for one hundred years wasn't exactly appealing.

To his left, Vincent saw at least five bodies connected in one way or another. He tipped his head, trying to figure out where one started and another ended.

How did…? Never mind.

Vincent continued walking, reminding himself why he was here. He was looking for Kate and half hoping she was, *and wasn't*, in the room. What would he do if he found her under a male?

His fists clenched.

Or even a female?

While that had *some* appeal, Vincent knew he had no right to be there looking for her.

If he saw her spread wide being licked, would he watch? Could he stand back and do nothing? His balls began to ache. Reaching inside his pants, he gripped his cock.

"Your Majesty," a female purred from the circular pool which was popular during the cooler months. The brown-haired vampire sat on the edge with her feet in the shallow water. "Come join us."

She was pretty. Flowing hair and big, matching brown eyes laced with mischief. He looked at her large breasts as she took hold of them, pinching her nipples. Another female giggled at him and slipped between the female's legs, beginning to lick her while glancing at him in invitation.

Jesus.

His mouth watered. He could just step up there and thrust his cock into Brown Eyes's mouth if he chose. Instead, he stood there stroking himself, his eyes darting between the two females.

No one would touch him first.

He was the king now. The rules had changed.

Brown Eyes rubbed her nipples between her fingers while the female between her legs vigorously sucked and lapped at her glistening flesh. She began to orgasm, never once taking her eyes off him.

He didn't want to come.

It felt wrong.

What the fuck is wrong with me?

Nothing, apparently, because when the female thrust her fingers inside Brown Eyes and her ecstasy reached a new level, his cock surged, and he let out a long groan as he released his seed over his hand.

Vincent stroked himself dry as an uneasy feeling spread throughout his chest.

Brown Eyes smiled at him, joy all over her face at pleasing her king.

Ugh.

He nodded at her, and saw the disappointment in her eyes moments before she covered it up with another smile.

This was why he didn't fucking want a line of goddamn females in his bed.

Tucking himself away, he looked up and decided to do a lap of the room before leaving. More eyes attempted to capture him and failed. As he reached the main door, he heard a group of female voices. Or rather, giggles.

The door pushed open and in walked four females.

One of them Kate.

She froze when she saw him.

So did he.

Dammit.

Her eyes narrowed, glanced around him as if displeased, and then returned to his.

She began to curtsy, and he walked the few paces to catch her arm. For some reason, he hated watching her lower herself to him, which was all kinds of crazy given it was their law and every single vampire had done so before him his entire life.

"Your Majesty," she started, staring at his hold on her arm. "Is everything alright?"

Christ, what am I doing?

He was manhandling her. Stopping her from curtsying in front of everyone.

He coughed.

"Yes, sorry, I thought you had tripped."

The females she had arrived with all lowered their eyes. They all knew he was lying but would never question their king.

Annoyed with himself, he tugged on her arm. "Walk with me," he ordered, ignoring the irritation in her eyes.

"Of course, Your Majesty," she said, turning her face away from him.

"Kate," he began, then found he could think of nothing to say.

"How was your day?" she asked instead as he looped her arm through his.

Christ. At this rate, they'd be talking about the weather next.

He missed the intimacy and ease they'd shared the night of his parents' vigil. Despite his grief, they had talked about their youths and fond memories.

"So there we were, chasing each other with real swords along the parapet at the top of the castle, and my mother was trying to stop us. Of course, Brayden had to be a complete show-off and jump from one to the other."

Kate had gasped.

"Did he fall? Your poor mother."

"He did fall." Vincent had laughed. *"And it took him days to heal. Of course, being a young vampire, it took longer than it would have now."*

Kate had shaken her head, smiling.

"He was always her favorite, though, so I think she secretly loved looking after him."

"I'm sure that's not true."

"She loved us both, but I spent most of my life shadowing the king and didn't spend half the time Brayden did with Mama." He shrugged. *"So it's only natural. I was closer to Papa."*

Kate had put her head in her hand and sighed. *"It's so strange to hear them being called that. They will always be King Frances and Queen Guiliana to me."*

Vincent had played that scene over and over in his head since that day. Kate had met his parents while they were still alive—her own parents well to do, so invited to court—but he wished he could take her to meet his mama so she could know her. Which was ridiculous.

Why would he want to do that?

Neither of the Moretti princes had ever brought a female to meet the queen. Not for any reason.

Kate had shared stories of growing up in Rome. She was a single child, her father a businessman in Italy, well connected and respected. It had struck him that she'd had a fairly lonely life with no sibling to dance around on rooftops with, but she seemed close to her parents. When he'd asked her why she had come to court this year with them, she'd been vague, but he felt she was hiding something.

In the end, it had been Vincent who had destroyed their closeness by apologizing for a kiss they'd shared in an attempt to show respect, which had only hurt her. He'd told her it wouldn't happen again and seen the moment the light in her eyes died.

He had hurt her.

Yet, he would only hurt her more if he took her to his chambers.

Vincent had to remain focused on cementing his role as king, on strengthening his race, and not on taking advantage of beautiful females. Or at least of Kate; no one else was of any interest whatsoever, and while Vincent was no playboy, not like the prince, it was odd. He'd concluded it was stress. Losing one's parents and becoming the king of an entire race was most likely considered high on the stress threshold, he was sure.

The fact he wanted to pull Kate's skirts up and fuck her brains out was irrelevant. Vincent was choosing to ignore that little technicality.

Goddamn it.

He really wanted to see her smile again and enjoy her

company.

If he couldn't bed her, then a little innocent flirting wouldn't harm anyone, would it?

"Oh, you know, I just sat on my throne and bossed everyone around," Vincent said, smiling down at her.

Kate blushed, and his entire world lit up.

"Sounds difficult, my lord." She smiled, teasing him back.

He grinned, staring ahead of them, feeling happier than he had in days.

"Very."

He led them outside the castle and through the gardens. The air was mild, and aside from a gardener in the distance, they had some privacy.

"And your parents, did they leave this eve?"

Vincent quickly lifted Kate off her feet as she caught her shoe on something. Her hand landed on his chest for a moment, their eyes meeting as he lowered her to her feet. He felt both their hearts begin to pound.

They could both hear it, but carried on walking.

"Ah, yes, they…yes, they did. Thank you," Kate replied, a little breathless. Then she stopped and turned to face him. "Can I ask you a question, sire?"

Vincent turned and glanced down into the most beautiful face he'd ever seen. If only she knew how much she took his breath away.

Better she didn't.

Her hair was piled on top of her head, and one or two strands were threatening to break loose. He suspected Kate would hate that, as she was always so perfectly put together. His fingers twitched to do something about it, but he didn't. Instead, he directed his attention to her pretty eyes as they darted around his face, awaiting his answer.

He smiled at her, loving this moment of anticipation between them.

God, he wanted to kiss her.

Suddenly, her lips parted gently. Forget kissing—he wanted those lips wrapped around his cock.

He saw the moment she recognized his need, and her own desire flickered across her face. She damn well licked her lips, and his mouth watered.

Stop.

Fuck.

Vincent ran a hand over the side of his face and got their conversation back on track. "Ask me," he ground out, his voice gruff.

Her eyes flashed.

He realized his mistake. He knew what Kate was going to ask.

She glanced back toward the castle. "Did you…in there…were you…?"

Shit.

Kate thought he was her mate. Regret lanced through him. How had he let it get to this? She was concerned he was being disloyal. A big part of him loved the strength and spirit she was exhibiting even just by asking him. And if she was *not* his mate, why was he so eager to tell her he had not?

"Partaking?" he asked. "No. Definitely not."

Definitely not? You moron.

Relief filled Kate's eyes as her face visibly relaxed.

Give her a reason why. Tell her it's not her.

He could think of nothing. The mix of emotions racing through him right now was confusing. He was relieved she was not worried he'd been with another female.

Vincent had no desire to hurt her in that way, even though he had no reason to feel disloyal—or be loyal. But he was also incredibly concerned that Kate was being misled.

By him.

He knew the right thing to do was to keep away from her. Put some distance between them. And yet, these walks, these chats, he lived for them. It's like they were his purpose.

Aside from being king.

Which, he reminded himself as he stared at her lips, was his priority.

CHAPTER FOUR

England 1891

Kate allowed the king to walk her back to her room. Just the feel of him under her hands had been intoxicating. And not because he was the king.

Because he was Vincent.

She knew she was falling in love with him. In her heart, she believed the king was her mate. It was such a strong and all-encompassing feeling, yet she could tell no one lest she look like a fool.

Worse, from Vincent, all she got in return was a bundle of mixed messages.

One minute, the king was being possessive, dragging her out of an orgy and staring at her like she was the most desirable female in the race; the next, he would dismiss her coldly. It had her head in a spin.

Every day, Kate would see him as they went about their lives. He would send her a smile and she'd blush. She had caught him watching her more than once during their main meal. And not just a small glance either; these were long moments where she could see him in a reflection or out of the corner of her eye. Kate would wait before eventually giving in and turning to him. He was never bashful about it. Vincent would give her a discreet wink and grin as she blushed.

He thought no one noticed, but they did. The prince would be watching them and give her an odd, small smile which felt like pity, but Kate was so sure Vincent was her mate, so she could be patient.

Because the thing was, Vincent Moretti was gorgeous. She loved talking to him and found him endlessly interesting, educated, and funny. But he was so goddamn sexy she had to stop herself from jumping him most days.

His tall, strong body was just calling her to touch him. Tonight, when he'd lifted her in his arms, saving her from tripping over a branch, had been swoon worthy. And she was not a female who swooned. Yet, when her hand had landed on his chest and she'd felt the layers of solid muscle, her panties had moistened. A low-level buzz remained running throughout her body, warm and needy.

"Are you okay?" Vincent asked as they arrived at her door.

"Mm-hmm," she replied, nodding.

He tilted her chin to make her look at him. Hope sprang within her as she glanced at his lips, waiting for him to lower his head and finally claim her.

A small groan left them instead, and Vincent moved an inch away. "Good day, Kate. May you rest well."

Goddamn him.

She needed his hands on her. Or they would need to be her own.

"It shall not be restful, my lord. I will tell you that," she muttered.

Kate didn't know what had come over her. The words had just fallen out.

Vincent frowned and stepped forward to open her door before all but pushing her inside. "Good day, Kate," he mumbled again and crossed his arms.

She mumbled *good day* and walked into her room. Flopping on the bed, she let out a long, loud groan.

Oh, how she ached for him.

That damn male had no idea how sexy he was.

Oh, those long, solid limbs of his. How she would love them between her own.

Vincent was tall and broad chested, as a king should be, with a strong jaw and dark, wavy hair. Though he kept it short, it was long enough to run your fingers through. Or so she imagined. His deep brown eyes saw everything, and when they weren't narrowed at her for one reason or another, they sparkled when he was teasing her.

And that damn wink of his.

Kate closed her eyes and imagined Vincent lying over her, heat enveloping them both as he stared down at her full of lust. With his shirt off, she could only imagine his round, solid shoulders and powerful arms on either side of her head as he made his way down her body to begin pleasing her.

Kate's hand bunched up her skirts, and she moaned as her fingers found the wetness that had been building. She circled her clit, imaging it was Vincent's hand instead of her own, and spread her legs.

"Oh, God," she quietly moaned. "Touch me."

She increased the speed, pulling her bodice down, exposing her breasts. As soon as the pink bud was pressed between her fingers, she let out a groan.

Would Vincent suck or bite her nipples as he tucked her legs up, widening the space for his big thighs so he could thrust inside her?

Kate rubbed and squeezed, seeing only the king as he fucked her pussy, totally filling her.

Heat flushed throughout her body as she arched into the imagined force of his touch.

"*Ohyesyesyes.*"

As her orgasm crashed beneath her fingers, she heard a bang. Sitting up, her fingers still in her wet flesh, she heard voices.

"*Vince, man, what are you doing?*"

"*Nothing. Fuck. Get out of here.*"

What in the blazes? Was the king outside her chambers?

Kate crossed the room and yanked open the door.

Vincent turned, and his eyes burned into hers. Her mouth dropped open as embarrassment burned on her cheeks.

"What—?" she began, but the king flew across the space between them, pushed her into the room, and slammed the door shut. The next moment she was up against the wall, and Vincent's lips slammed down on hers. His mouth possessed her while his hand ran up her body and took hold of her breast.

"I can smell you," he growled against her lips, then plowed his tongue in deeper.

Kate felt him hard against her stomach and knew he was ready for her. She began to reach for him, but he grabbed her wrist, pulling her a few inches away.

"Don't do that again," he said.

When Kate glanced at her hand, Vincent shook his

head. "No. Not that. Well, yes, that. But I mean…" He looked over at her bed.

He wanted her to stop masturbating?

She narrowed her eyes at him.

"Now you are being ridiculous, Vincent."

In here, he was Vincent. Out there, he was the king. Only the two of them knew the distinction.

"I know. Just…*fuck*, I need to go." He stared at her mouth for a long moment, cursed again, then left.

Kate sighed.

Eventually, he would realize she was his mate. Wouldn't he?

CHAPTER FIVE

England, 1891

I shouldn't have kissed her.
I shouldn't have listened at the door.
I shouldn't have…

"That poor fucking female," Brayden said, interrupting his thoughts.

Craig followed the prince into his office while Vincent ignored their chatter. God only knew which female, human or otherwise, the two of them were rambling on about now.

He stood up from the small sofa in his office and began to walk across the room.

"Kate? Yeah, poor girl," Craig replied.

What?

Vincent stopped, turned, and narrowed his eyes at them.

"What's wrong with Kate?"

"Don't be an ass, brother," Brayden chided, leaning his hand against the wall. "That gorgeous female wants you. Instead of servicing her, you left her to pleasure herself while you jerked off at her door."

So much for brotherly loyalty. The little fucker had told Craig? Sometimes, being king was a pain in the ass. Like now, when he wanted to throw a punch at the prince's damn face.

"I was not jerking off. I was…protecting her," he growled.

They both laughed at him.

Fuck's sakes.

"Why doesn't Kate come to the day parties?" Craig asked, shrugging. "Plenty of vampires in there who would *protect* her while she's finding her happy place."

Day parties? What was this, a mother's group?

"Orgies," Vincent sneered. "Call them what they are, for goodness' sake."

"Fine. The fuck-fests." Craig grinned.

Brayden crossed his arms, ignoring the commander, and frowned at him. "Wait a minute. Have you told Kate she can't attend the orgies?"

"Fuck-fests. We've rebranded." Craig snorted.

Vincent shook his head.

He knew what the two of them were up to. Since they'd met, Craig and Brayden had been tight friends; it was like having a second annoying little brother. Together, they loved winding him up, even though he was now the goddamn king.

It was, besides sex, their favorite past time.

When it came to Kate, Vincent wasn't having it. She was not a toy to be played with. They could find another topic to wind him up about.

"I have not," Vincent replied, crossing his arms despite the fact he wasn't telling the entire truth. He may have lost his shit several weeks ago, which had gone down…well, not very well at all. But he hadn't *banned* her. Unless asking a few of his soldiers to advise him if Kate showed up at one of the events was considered *banning*.

Tomayto, tomahto.

"In any case, Kate is a female of class and isn't the type to frequent such places."

"You mean classy like the duchess and princess who attended yesterday?" Craig asked, laughing.

That wasn't a big surprise. Royalty—human royalty—had been known to attend from time to time. Though they always had to have their minds wiped.

Vincent groaned. "Dammit. Stop inviting them. And make sure you clean up their memories before they leave. I don't want any leakage on my watch."

Brayden rolled his eyes. "He's the commander of your army, Vincent. As if he's going to let anyone who poses a risk leave the property. Now, back to Kate."

"*Not* back to Kate; she's no one's business," he growled, ignoring their grins.

Fuckers.

Vincent walked to his desk and sat down, switching to king mode. His fingers entwined as he laid them on the surface in front of him, and their smiles faded.

"So, what did you want to see us about?" Brayden asked.

About fucking time.

It was his turn to grin. "We're moving to America."

And…totally worth the wait to see their smart-assed mouths fall open.

CHAPTER SIX

Present Time

"I really don't know if this is a good idea, Vince," Brayden said as he rubbed his hand over his jaw again. "Not to question your judgment, but it makes me nervous."

Vincent slapped him on the back, and they continued walking through the castle.

"It'll be fine. It's only a small number of the *Operation Daylight* team. It's about opening up and showing them who we are, and that we're no threat to them. Showing. Not telling them. Of course, I expect you to arrange our best security for their arrival."

Operation Daylight was the name given to the team of world leaders who were aware of their existence.

All their lives, they'd lived among humans undetected until a letter sent to the president of the United States and a leak from his office had seen the information go viral. The Moretti team had been able to counter it with a *fake news* campaign on social media, and so far, it had worked. But for how long, they didn't know. For now, Vincent was focused on educating the *Operation Daylight* team about the vampire race and eradicating as much fear about them as possible. They'd already seen how humans behaved when they discovered something they didn't understand. Dozens of his vampires had been kidnapped and tested on in the labs. It had rightfully infuriated him, but he'd turned his anger into fuel.

Now, Vincent was determined to lay a solid foundation of trust with these humans so nothing like that happened ever again. Fortunately, many of them weren't strangers. The Morettis had rubbed shoulders with the elite and powerful around the world for centuries.

"Hell yeah, they will be," Craig said behind him.

Vincent didn't doubt his security team; they were the most powerful in the race.

"I see the benefits in doing this," Lance spoke. "They'll see we're just like them."

"Sure, just bigger, stronger, and faster." Kurt laughed.

Vincent stopped as they reached the foyer in the front entrance of his castle. He eyed a whole bunch of sparkly shit. Turning as he stepped through the archway, he spotted an enormous Christmas tree.

And that wasn't all.

Underneath it were at least fifty thousand gift boxes. The entire foyer was lined with fairy lights winding up the staircase banisters and mistletoe hanging in doorways. In one corner, there was a group of smaller trees, as if the larger one had given birth to triplets.

"What the fuck," he cursed loudly. "Did Santa throw up in here?"

"I think the—"

Before Brayden could finish, the door burst open, and four familiar females came inside, giggling as they removed their jackets. All of whom came to a screeching halt when they saw them.

Cue the guilty eyes darting at each other.

Then, as if they'd rehearsed it, they each began to smile sexily at their mates.

Vincent frowned, not making eye contact with Kate.

"Hey, baby." Brianna danced over to Craig and tossed herself into his chest.

Vincent shook his head.

Are you kidding me?

"What are you females up to?" Lance asked, tugging Sofia into his side.

"A good question, De Luca," Vincent said, narrowing his eyes at Willow, who refused to look at him.

"We were just going for a walk, darling," Kate replied as she waddled up to him (her words, not his), and he placed his hands on her belly. He caught her eye for a moment, sharing a private moment as they acknowledged their growing child.

Then he glanced around at the chaos.

"In the hail?" He frowned and she shrugged.

He didn't believe a word of it.

Bang.

"It's all lit up, Miss Brianna!" one of their tech guys announced as he bounded through the door, doing the same coat removal dance, freezing when he saw the king.

Suddenly, everyone began talking. The techie mumbling *Your Majesty* as he lowered his head. The males groaning and rubbing their foreheads. The females offering to make him his favorite drink and directing him into the library.

Did they think he was stupid?

"Stop!" he ordered.

There was silence as they all held their breath.

Vincent groaned as he thought about how best to deal with this. These females were out of control with their antics. He knew that if he walked through his front door, his blood pressure would shoot through the roof. Part of him wanted to turn around and walk away, but the old "give them an inch and they'll take a mile" philosophy kept his feet right where they were.

He loved how his queen had female company. He was pleased that his brother had his mate and that many of the other males were coupling up.

But this was a goddamn castle. A *working* royal castle.

"Willow bought the baby a drum set for Christmas!" Brianna suddenly announced.

Everyone turned to stare at her.

"It's from Santa! Could have been anyone…" Willow growled.

Beside him, Kate was giggling.

Brayden cursed.

"Are we buying gifts? Like humans?" Lance asked, sounding genuinely interested.

Vincent rolled his eyes and sighed.

"Ladies, if I step outside these doors, what am I going to see?"

A bunch of *oh, well,* and *some decorations,* and *bit of tinsel* sounded around him.

"Which required the help of a technician, did it?"

Craig groaned.

"What did you do?" Craig asked, tipping Brianna's chin. "Did you buy the big set? I said no."

Set of? Set of fucking what?

What the hell had these females done to the front entrance of his castle?

"That's it." Vincent marched to the large double doors as four females ran after him crying out.

"You said he never comes out here!" Brianna cried.

"Well, he normally doesn't," Kate answered, and he turned to glare at his mate.

Whipping open the doors, Vincent stepped out into the drizzle and stopped dead in his tracks. His mouth dropped open.

"Did I just step foot inside a fucking Christmas movie?"

"You watch Christmas movies?" Bri asked with a sparkle in her eye.

"No, I don't watch…never mind." He turned and pointed to the scene in front of him. "I said NO reindeer, and we never discussed life-size candy canes. And…good God. The giant Santa needs to go before I behead him."

"You got snow delivered?" Brayden asked, glancing at Craig with a frown. "How did we not know this was happening?"

"It's a machine. We hired it," Kate answered as if her answer was obvious.

"Actually, I knew about it. I thought you'd signed it off," Kurt said, narrowing his eyes at Brianna, who smiled back. "It's been running for a few hours."

Vincent crossed his arms and stared from one face to the other.

"Oh, come on. It's not like we snuck in half the rebellion," Kate huffed, frowning. "Come on, Vincent. It's Christmas."

He rolled his eyes so hard his head nearly fell off. "And we are v-a-m-p-i-r-e-s!" Vincent said before walking back inside.

They all followed.

"We have a handful of world leaders coming in a few days. It gives the wrong impression. Tone it down." He looked pointedly at Brianna. "No snow. No candy canes. No Santa."

He turned and marched off.

"*Yes!* He didn't mention the reindeer," Brianna squeaked.

"NO reindeer!" he yelled without turning, mostly because he didn't want them to see his grin.

"Drat."

Vincent walked into the operations room a few hours later.

The senior lieutenant commanders sat haphazardly around the room, as they always did, while Craig and Brayden leaned on their desks up the front of the room.

"Let's double security in the morning and get the black team prepped for the *Operation Daylight* guests arrival," Craig instructed his guys after nodding his head at the king in acknowledgement of his arrival. "Bray and I will be with the king, but I want you four monitoring every inch of the property and beyond."

"From this point onward," Brayden added.

"Out about two miles?" Tom asked.

Craig nodded as he turned to the map on the screen behind them. "Yup, should be fine."

"I'm not expecting any issues," Vincent spoke, leaning against the wall and crossing his arms. "I understand their security guys will be here to spec the place the night before."

"I'll be leading that," Craig confirmed. "But I want you all across it, so check your tablets on the regular."

"Just the POTUS team, right?" Marcus asked, and Craig shook his head.

"All of them, so we will deal with each team separately. I'm not having security experts running around the place unsupervised."

They all nodded.

Vincent rarely interfered with these issues. Brayden was the captain of his army and Craig the commander. Together, they had worked effectively for centuries, well before he had taken the throne. Even the four senior lieutenant commanders had been in their roles for hundreds of years. It was a well-oiled machine, and they were as loyal as any king could ask for.

Their number one job was protecting him and the queen, then the prince and princess (yes, there was a conflict of interest, given Bray was the captain, but he knew the drill, and Craig was quick to remind him when he hesitated), then the vampire race.

All of it.

"I see Diego Lombardo is not on the list," Lance mentioned, crossing his arms.

The Italian president had been found to be in bed, so to speak, with Stefano Russo. They were still uncovering exactly how deep his involvement with the rebellion leader was, but it wasn't good. They believed he had played a part in the kidnapping and testing of his vampires. After Vincent's private conversation with the POTUS a few months ago, they had both realized it was impossible to have him arrested or removed. They couldn't expose his activities without going public about the vampire race.

Still, a leader could be in power and have very little.

"He's been removed from *Operation Daylight*," Vincent informed. "And silenced, as much as we can. President Adler assures me Lombardo won't be a problem. I'd love to know what they have on him, but no, that fucker is not stepping foot on Moretti land. And never will."

Lance nodded a few times. It had been his mate, Sofia, who had gone into those labs and first seen the captured vampires lying helplessly on the laboratory beds.

"Okay, any questions?" Brayden asked, glancing at his watch. When everyone shook their heads, the team was dismissed. As the room cleared, the prince glanced over at him. "What's up?"

"I want you to take part in this tour when the leaders arrive. Officially. As a royal."

"Why?"

Vincent was expecting the question.

As captain of the army, Brayden never got involved with royal duties. He focused on security and leading his team, not schmoozing with society. He knew the prince hated the fluffy royal stuff, as he called it, and their mother had often pushed back when their father had insisted.

Vincent had never seen any reason to change that for as long as he'd been king. The structure they'd had until now was a good one. Aside from a brief time earlier in the year when they thought he was dying, Vincent had been happy for the prince to continue being captain and leading their security.

But now things were different.

The strength and visibility of the royal family needed to be a priority.

"Times have changed, Bray. I want to ensure you have

a relationship with these people. You are the prince, which as they come to understand our way of life, they'll realize is a prominent position. Willow should also attend as princess," he explained. "We're a royal family, and one day, that will be public knowledge around the world. We should start off as we mean to go on."

"Fuck me," Brayden said, staring at him.

"I'm sure your mate will be more excited than you are." He laughed.

"Because of the dinner."

Not a question. They both knew Willow would love dressing up. All the females would. And some of the males.

"Fancy as fuck," Vincent answered, nodding "Wear your best stuff."

"I'm still wearing my weapons," Brayden muttered, crossing his arms.

"I'd expect nothing less."

CHAPTER SEVEN

Present Time

Kate leaned her head back against the custom shaped cushions and let the jets of the enormous spa bath massage her body. The baby moved within her, happy to be immersed in water. This little one was likely to be a swimmer, she surmised.

She couldn't wait to meet her child.

Unlike humans, they couldn't just go get a sonogram and find out the sex of the baby. The heart rate would immediately draw the sonographer's attention to something not being right, and while they could wipe their memories, the digital footprint was just too complex. Even if the technician was a vampire, the risks of leaving a trail were just not worth it.

Vampire pregnancies were rare, and because they didn't get sick, the need for medical support wasn't the same as for humans. She had a midwife for delivery, but the female was a vampire.

She loved the hours Vincent and she had lain trying to guess the sex of the baby and teasing each other about it. One day he wanted a little prince, and the next a little princess. He had every reason for and against listed for either option, and would circle around to them again and again. In the end, Vincent had decided a son would be better because he would never let a male lay a finger on his daughter.

She didn't doubt it.

Kate adored listening to Vincent talk about their baby. He was already so in love with it.

One day he'd asked her to show him how to change a diaper, so she'd grabbed the closest teddy bear, a diaper from the beautiful wooden dresser, and led him to the changing table. A short time later, the bear and four diapers had been flung across the room, and Vincent had muttered something about bears shitting in the woods, planted a kiss on her lips, and stalked out.

She had hidden her smile.

"My beautiful mate," Vincent spoke, surprising her. He placed a gentle kiss on her lips and sat on the edge of the bath.

"Join me," she said, taking in the large male that was all hers. His hair was askew as if he'd run his hands through it recently, and his jaw was scattered with dark hair. Tonight, he was dressed in a pair of dark blue jeans with a black shirt slightly open at the neck and rolled at the sleeves.

Damn, he was sexy.

Vincent slipped his hand into the water and cupped one of her breasts, a slight question on his face. She was tender tonight, but it felt nice to have his hands on her.

They had both been so busy, and she'd been sleeping a lot.

"I only have a few minutes," he said, shaking his head. "I was coming to tell you Seraphina is taking care of the dinner event for our guests, so you can take that job off your list."

Kate was a hands-on kind of queen. While she ran the household with a large staff, she was often involved with much more than a human queen would be. It was just the way it was. Looking back, Kate realized she'd taken it all on because of the lack of female company. When Seraphina had joined the household, she had become a friend. Kate had no doubt the female would do a wonderful job.

"That's fine. Thank you."

She glanced down into the water as Vincent's hand moved from her breast and over her belly. Her eyes darted to his, and he ventured further.

"Don't you dare start and then disappear," she warned.

He leaned down and growled against her lips. "I wouldn't dare, my queen." His thumb found her clit and began circling it.

She groaned.

Two fingers slipped inside her pussy, and she arched into his hand.

"Fuck my fingers, Kate," he ordered in a soft growl. "You don't need much right now, do you, sweetheart?"

She hated that he was right. Her body was so sensitive it was like a firecracker when he touched her.

"Touch your breasts," he ordered again, and the next minute, she was cupping them and pinching her hard nipples.

Vincent continued his finger work. In and out he massaged, her clit burning with delight. He was an expert after so many years, knowing the exact way to pleasure her.

"Fuck, yes, that's it. Good girl. Come for me." He groaned.

Kate began to pant, water splashing everywhere.

"Yes, God, *yesssss*."

Vincent's lips swallowed her cry as he thrust three fingers inside her, milking her orgasm completely.

When she opened her eyes, her king had pulled his cock out of his pants.

"Take me in your mouth."

Kate sat forward and licked the precum, running his cock over her lips as she stared up at him.

"In your mouth, now, Kate," he growled.

God, she loved how bossy he was. It got her hot and aroused all over again.

Smiling, she wrapped a hand around him and began to lick him like a lollipop. That lasted about five seconds before he directed her head and pushed himself inside her mouth. Working him with her tongue and lips, in and out, she loved how hard and smooth he was. She wrapped her fingers around his sack and sucked his cock.

"Yes, fuck, swallow for me, sweetheart," Vincent said as heat filled her throat.

She lay back, wiping her thumb across her lips, gazing at her god of a male.

Kate watched as he cleaned up and put himself away. Her eyes began to droop.

"Come here." Vincent lifted her out of the bath and wrapped her in a thick white robe. "You'll fall asleep in there."

As he laid her in their bed and pulled the covers over

her, Kate felt like the most loved and cherished female in the world.

"Thank you, baby," she said as he ran a hand over her forehead.

"Don't thank me for loving you," he replied. "The pleasure is all mine."

She always did, because she'd never forget that he very nearly hadn't.

CHAPTER EIGHT

England, 1891

Vincent timed it perfectly.

He walked out of the dining hall and along the corridor, under the archway, and out into the garden.

"Kate," he said as if it was a coincidence to bump into her.

"Your Majesty," she replied politely, dropping a curtsy as if he hadn't had his tongue down her throat several days ago.

He'd tried to keep away, but not seeing her was driving him mad.

While he was busy making plans to move the royal household to America, Vincent's mind kept wandering to the feeling of Kate's soft skin under his hands and the feel of her warm body against his. In truth, he'd expected her to seek him out. When she hadn't, he'd wondered how she was feeling. Or if she felt anything.

During a meal a few days ago, he'd looked at her and found her watching him. She'd blushed, and his body had lit up. He had smiled and turned to find Craig and Brayden grinning like a bunch of idiots at him.

Had they stopped there?

No. Of course they hadn't.

"*I've heard the bigger the throne, the shorter the cock. Maybe she'd prefer a longer one?*" Idiot One had said as he'd walked into a room a few hours later.

They'd heard him coming; he wasn't stupid.

"*You've seen my cock, dumbass,*" he'd responded, not in the least concerned he was lacking.

"*If you aren't going to make a move, for God's sakes, let some other males enjoy those juicy globes,*" Brayden had said, risking his life.

Vincent had sped across the room and held his brother by the neck. The grin on the prince's face hadn't deterred him, but he'd dropped him a moment later.

"*I told you all,*" he said, turning around. "*Kate is off-limits. Now get back to fucking work.*"

He'd waited a few more days, and she still hadn't made any move to seek him out or cross his path. Vincent had even wandered into another orgy in a huff, only to storm out and slam the door shut when he found she wasn't there. Brayden had given him shit about it, and he couldn't blame him. Talk about wrecking the sexy vibe.

But whatever. He had been frustrated, so he had finally given in and put himself in her path.

Now she stood in front of him looking gorgeous as ever with all her flowing blonde hair. Tonight, she wore a blue dress which made her eyes pop, and with the skirt cinched at her waist, the fitting bodice emphasized her more-than-a-handful breasts.

He imagined she would be displeased if he were to rip open her dress and expose them, but that was exactly what he wanted to do, then suckle on her nipples until she cried.

"Are you well?" she asked, interrupting his thoughts.

"Hmm? Oh, yes," he replied, returning his eyes to her beautiful face. "Walk with me."

Kate swallowed and nodded, taking his arm.

Vincent led them out into the garden until they were out of earshot from other vampires. They'd covered all the pleasantries: *Beautiful night. Yes. Lovely meal. Was she enjoying her time at the castle?*

Blah, blah, blah.

Trying to ignore his semihard cock, Vincent placed his hand over hers, which was looped around his bicep, and squeezed it. "I wanted to apologize for the other day."

Kate blinked, and her luscious lips parted in surprise.

Vincent thought he saw a hint of sadness in her eyes. He was very aware Kate was attracted to him, but hadn't they also become friends of sorts? Didn't she know he didn't do this sort of thing? Pulling a female aside like this drew attention no matter how subtle he was about it. Yet, he cared for her, and it was important to him that he apologize for his actions and apologize for his past behavior.

Even though he really wanted to do it again.

His gaze was drawn to her bodice, where his fingers itched to push the fabric down and free her breasts. God, he wanted those globes in his mouth. His cock twitched and hardened further.

Vincent looked across the garden and closed his eyes in an attempt to push back the arousal rushing through him. Her little nails pressed into his arms, and he looked down at her.

"You're apologizing?"

"Yes, because—"

"Are you not attracted to me?" Kate turned into him, and he could see her nipples through the fabric of her dress, her breathing heavy as hooded eyes took in his powerful chest.

Fuck.

She was offering herself to him. Out here in the evening where he could lay her down in the grass and lift her dress, then plunge his thick, heavy cock inside her. A tightness in his balls sent a zing up his spine when she laid a hand on his pec.

Fuck me.

Perhaps he'd flip her and take her from behind as he took hold of her large, soft breasts.

Heavy lashes flickered as her eyes moved over his body, reaching his face. She smiled sensually at him, and he felt the precum on the end of his fat crown. If she dropped to her knees and pulled him out right fucking now, he'd be powerless to say no. Just the thought of her mouth sliding over his swollen cock made him want to press in deeper.

Wait. Had he just thrust against her?

Kate licked her lips, and he became transfixed with the glistening moisture it left. Lowering his face, he…

Fuck.

His eyes squeezed shut, and Kate moved an inch away.

"Do not misunderstand me, Kate."

"It's fine, my lord. I understand," she said, the heat within her still rich in her throat.

God, she must be wet for him.

They stared at each other with such need, and yet, neither moved. He couldn't. He had nothing to offer her except his thick cock. Yet, he couldn't let go of her completely.

Kate finally looked away, her cheeks rosy from arousal, but he also saw shame.

He had to explain.

No one knew what he was dealing with. Vincent had always known being king would be lonely. Very few, if any, ever truly understood. *It's lonely at the top*, words his father had said to him over and over again. He still had much to learn. He had a long road ahead of him to ensure his vampires trusted he was the right male for the job. Sure, it was his birthright, but like any leader, you were only as powerful as those who chose to follow you.

But it was also more than that.

He wanted this job. He cared about his vampires. Every time he woke, he pledged to protect all of them and ensure his race thrived.

"Kate. Please, I don't think you do," Vincent said, his eyes running over her. "You are so fucking…you take my breath away. But right now, I have a kingdom to rule. A race to protect. Having a female…"

Christ, could he finish a damn sentence?

"Of course," she interrupted, her eyes turning empty. "The throne is your priority."

Vincent saw her disappointment, not in the situation but in him, and it hurt more than he had expected it to.

"I'd like you to stay. At court," he added quickly.

Kate blinked in surprise.

"I…in what capacity, my lord? I am due to return home at the end of the season. Soon. In a few short weeks," she said, a little breathless.

It was a good question.

Come on, Vincent. What capacity?

Fuck me.

It had just fallen out. He had no right to ask this of her, yet the thought of her leaving was unacceptable. Totally and overwhelmingly unacceptable. His chest tightened the more he thought about it.

Then he realized he had more to tell her. Not only did he want her to stay but he also wanted her to come with him.

"I am moving the royal household to America. I will be announcing it tomorrow," he told her as her eyebrows shot up. "I want you to join us, Kate."

Her mouth opened and closed a few times, all fishlike, as he waited for her answer. While imagining his cock moving in and out of her plump red lips.

"Vincent," she started, shaking her head. "I cannot. My family is in Italy; my home is there."

He stifled back a growl from deep within his throat.

Vincent couldn't let her leave. A powerful need to possess her overtook him. He took a step forward, placing a hand on her hip, and felt her tremble against him as he pulled her against his body. "Kate, I must have you."

"Yes," she replied, arching her neck and back, pressing her breasts into him.

Vincent took one in his hand and began to pull the material away. Kate's breath hitched, and the pink of her areola became visible.

His mouth watered.

His head lowered.

Kate's stiff pink nipple was now exposed as she moaned in his arms.

"Yes, touch me," she pleaded.

His tongue reached out and licked across the hard peak, then his mouth latched on, sucking as Kate fisted his hair. He bunched up her dress, his hand making its way toward the burning heat at her core. He smiled as her legs moved apart.

God, she was going to be such a sweet lover.

"You...we must...tell others. Announce this," Kate panted. "If I stay."

Vincent froze.

He lifted his head and took in her flushed face. She was ready to be fucked. His cock was hard as a rock and ready to thrust inside this female.

Announce it?

No, he wasn't going to announce that he'd fucked Kate.

But that wasn't what she meant.

She thought she would be queen. She thought she was his mate.

And this was what he'd been wary of.

This was lust. For him at least. Kate was a beautiful and graceful vampire who he felt protective of. He cared for her. It wasn't more than that. He was sure of it.

He had to stay focused on the throne, on his new job as the new king.

Vincent cupped her cheeks, lifting her face so her eyes met his. Her plump red lips quivered as she readied to meet them. When he lowered his head, a small hand landed on his chest. He narrowed his eyes in question.

"You do not intend to make an announcement, do you?"

He squeezed his eyes as if in pain.

"Kate," he began. "I cannot stay away from you. I cannot stop thinking of you. Yet, the throne must come first."

When she made to move away from him, Vincent was desperate to make her understand. His role was not something he could walk away from. He was the king of an entire race of vampires. Did no one understand the pressure he was under to live up to his father's and grandfather's past success?

They had been great kings.

He had to be a great king.

"Please, Kate," he said. "I must have you."

"Let me go, Vincent. I will not be your lover," she replied, hurt mixed with need in her voice.

He stared at her, frowning.

"Only my mate can become queen, Kate. You know this."

Kate nodded and glanced away.

Did Kate think she was his mate?

Irritation blazed within him. It was completely unreasonable of him, he knew. The need to possess and protect her overwhelmed him. He released her from his arms and took a step away.

"This is why I do not take lovers," he muttered, running a hand through his already tousled hair. "It sends the wrong message, and females start forming expectations."

"Expectations?" Kate asked, her voice rising.

"Yes." He turned and faced her ire. "Expectations. I cannot *make* you my mate."

"How do you know I am not?"

He began to splutter.

Kate glanced at his erection.

"You think a hard cock means you are my mate?" He frowned. "Kate, I may want to plunge inside you, fill you with my seed, but I cannot guarantee you are my mate."

"You won't even try," she accused, lifting the material back over her breasts, and he swallowed hard. She frowned at his reaction and turned to leave.

Vincent grabbed Kate's arm, spun her around, and

slammed his lips down on hers. He forced his tongue inside as they both groaned, pressing their bodies together.

Their lips separated, and they stared at each other, gasping.

"I want to fuck you," Vincent demanded.

"No."

He needed more. He needed her naked on his bed, underneath him, where she would be safe and protected. And available for his cock day and night.

"Kate, I need you with me," he commanded gruffly.

She shook her head gently.

"You can't ask that of me," she replied. "You won't even try to see what this is."

Goddammit.

Vincent squeezed his eyes closed.

He had to stop.

When he lifted his lids and her pleading eyes caught his, he knew he had to let her go, because the day his mate did show up, he would hurt Kate beyond anything she was feeling now.

He wouldn't do that to her.

He tried to step away, but his body wouldn't move.

Vincent cupped her face.

"Just try..." Kate's small voice reached into his heart.

He stared back at her, opening his mouth to reply, when they heard the fast-approaching sound of footsteps.

Vincent released her.

Kate straightened herself as the young male stopped, panted, bowed, and turned to face Kate.

"Excuse me, Your Highness. Miss Valentino, there is a Mr. Riccardo Bocci here for you."

Who the hell is Riccardo Bocci?

Vincent's blood began to boil at the idea of a suitor

coming to see her. With her parents back in Italy, it was absolutely unsuitable. Mostly. They weren't human, of course, so their societal rules didn't exactly apply to vampires, but Vincent felt he should act as a protector of sorts for Kate.

It was totally inappropriate.

Unacceptable.

He wouldn't stand for it.

"He says he needs to speak with you urgently."

"Riccardo is here? At court?" Kate asked, her eyes flying open in surprise. "What for?"

Hearing Kate's heart rate increase caused Vincent's fists to clench. This male was important to her. He decided right there and then he would kill him.

Probably.

"He didn't say, milady. I have put him in the parlor, but he insisted I interrupt you and the king immediately."

Vincent raised a brow. This male thought he could decide whether the king was interrupted? And steal Kate away from him?

Not fucking likely.

"Tell Mr. Bocci he does not choose whether he can interrupt the king. Kate will be there when we are finished," Vincent growled.

The vampire lowered his head, and Vincent immediately felt like an asshole.

Probably because he was being an asshole. But it was this exact behavior which told him he did not yet have the respect of his vampires. No one would have fucking dared do such a thing to Frances Moretti, his father.

Kate went to reply, but he held up his hand.

"Go. Tell him we will be there promptly."

The vampire disappeared.

Kate glared at him, then lifted the hem of her skirts and began walking back to the castle.

Vincent stopped her. "Who is Mr. Bocci?"

"A male from home. A close friend of my family," she answered, taking a few steps in the direction of the castle.

"A suitor? Is he your mate?" Vincent asked, growling as he walked beside her.

"It has been expected we would mate, but has not yet happened," she replied. "I must go to him. It's strange he has come for me. Perhaps my father is calling me home early."

He grabbed her arm.

"I forbid it," he growled.

Kate stopped and turned to him in question.

Fuck.

"Kate, I told you I need you," he said as calmly as possible.

"It's unacceptable for me to go with you without a purpose, Vincent. You know that. I would be seen as nothing more than some concubine. My family would be embarrassed." She glanced at him. "And we both know it's more than that."

He stared at her, blinking.

"But if you do not see or feel that, I should return home," Kate added sadly. "I must go."

She surprised him by teleporting back to the castle.

Vincent stood in the cold, void space Kate had left behind and felt like someone had stabbed his heart with an ice pick. There was no way he could let her leave. Somehow, he had to convince her to stay.

To come with him to America.

Something told him he would be unhappy without her, so he had to figure out what she needed to stay. If he

could just get her on his cock, then perhaps she would.
  And yes, that made him an asshole.

CHAPTER NINE

England, 1981

Kate teleported back to the castle and ran through the halls to the parlor. She caught her breath, ran her hands over her dress, and tidied her hair before stepping inside the room.

Riccardo turned. Sad, anguished eyes met hers. He was across the room the next second, gripping her shoulders. "Kate, my God."

"Riccardo, how lovely to see you," she greeted, taken aback by his behavior. "Has my father—"

"Kate, sit," he interrupted, steering her to the sofa, sitting next to her. "I have news. Your—"

Vincent came barging into the room. Riccardo leapt to his feet, his mouth falling open before he bowed. "Your Majesty!"

Kate was well aware Riccardo had never been to court nor met the king or any of the royals before.

"Your name?" the king asked, standing with his hands on his hips, glaring at the vampire.

She frowned.

Vincent knew who Riccardo was.

His behavior was that of a mating vampire, yet he continued to deny his feelings. The lust and need between them was so thick, her own undergarments were wet as she sat here. Worse, as she stared at the male, her sex gently throbbed, needing him to taste her, fill her, touch her.

God, he was infuriating.

Vincent's eyes met hers and flared. They were both aware of the powerful desire for each other's bodies.

Suddenly, the prince entered the room, glancing from one face to the other.

"Your Royal Highness," Riccardo said, bowing again at Brayden, looking at her in desperation. Finally, he answered the king. "I am Riccardo Bocci. I need to speak to Kate in private, if I may, sire?"

Vincent crossed his arms.

"Anything you say to her, you may say in my presence."

"Or we could wait outside," Brayden suggested, raising a brow at his brother.

"No. I am fine right here," Vincent replied, taking a seat and waving his hand for Riccardo to do the same.

Kate sighed.

She glanced at his crotch, taking in the semihard cock in his pants, and he tilted his head at her. She blushed and glanced away.

Riccardo cleared his throat.

Brayden crossed his arms and leaned against the wall.

"Ricky, it's fine. Tell me what you are doing here," she prompted, patting the seat on the sofa beside her.

Riccardo's eyes flicked from one royal to the other as he sat.

She laid a hand on his arm and heard the king growl. Kate glared at him, and he returned it with one of his own.

"It's about your parents," Riccardo replied, placing a hand over hers. "They are dead."

"Fuck," Vincent cursed as an anguished cry left her throat.

CHAPTER TEN

Present Time

"I don't want you to do anything tonight," Vincent instructed.

He pulled on a jacket and held up a couple of ties, trying to decide on a color. He didn't really give a fuck, so he tossed one onto the bench, selecting the red one.

It was a powerful choice.

His blue suit was more welcoming than black, but still spoke of strength.

Okay, so perhaps he gave some fucks.

"Once we've greeted our guests, I want you to come back here and put your feet up until dinner, alright?"

Vincent watched Kate rub the side of her stomach as she lay among the one hundred and fifty thousand pillows on their enormous bed, or so it felt like when he tried to get into the damn bed each day.

"Vince, do you think this child of ours is going to

come early?" Kate asked him for the hundredth time in two days. He was beginning to wonder if she was doing that instinctual mom thing. He doubted she was aware just how many times she'd asked him, so he was now doubling down on the protective mate and daddy thing.

In other words, he wasn't taking any chances on their safety. The last thing they needed was the queen going into labor while they had a bunch of fucking humans in the castle.

Bray, he telepathed the prince.
Yup.
Make sure Willow stays with Kate tonight.
What's up?
Just a precaution.
Fuck off. I need more information.

Vincent stared at his reflection in the mirror and rolled his eyes. Although, he was being unfair. Brayden was in charge of the security for the royal family—even though he was a royal himself—and his comment would have sent warning bells through the warrior's brain.

There is a chance the queen is close to going into labor. Today, next week. I don't fucking know. I don't want her alone from now on.

Roger that. Leave it to me.

No doubt all the females would be on a roster within the next ten minutes, and Kate would want to strangle him. She was a very independent female, but that was too bad. The protection of her and their baby was his priority.

Nothing else mattered.

Well, that wasn't true.

The throne and the protection of the race was always there fighting for first place. It had nearly come between them once, in the beginning, and he would never let that happen again.

Every single day it was a fine line he balanced, but it was worth it. She was worth it.

"Maybe, my love," he answered. "But we're prepared. You have bought enough teddy bears and diapers, so we are ready."

She rolled her eyes at him and laughed. "Get over the bears already."

"Well, at least they're not bloody reindeers," he fake growled.

"You love them." Kate grinned.

"I do not love them, but I will tolerate them. Just don't tell *that* girl."

"Brianna."

"I know." He winked at her.

"I know you know," she said and laughed.

"Promise me you will rest while I host our guests until dinner," Vincent requested, leaning over her and propping an arm on the headboard.

Kate gazed up at him, a sexy twinkle in her eye.

"Behave," he gruffly said with a smirk.

"I will. Honestly, my energy is waning so quickly these days that your wish is granted, my darling." She accepted his lingering kiss. "Help me to my feet."

Vincent scooped her up and placed his mate on her feet, kissing her forehead.

Ten minutes later, Vincent was standing in Santa Central, also known as the entrance to his damn castle, with Kate by his side. Around him were the most powerful warriors of the race: Brayden, Craig, and the SLCs.

He heard the crunch of tires and turned to watch dozens of black bulletproof vehicles drive down the long driveway.

"The eagle has landed," Craig said.

Vincent glanced at the commander and raised a brow.

"What? I've always wanted to say that," Craig replied, shrugging with a nearly imperceptible smirk.

Brayden snorted.

All of them had comms shoved in their ears, and Vincent could see the others talking to their teams, who were scattered in and around the castle.

Kate moved a tiny inch closer to him, and he casually moved his arm behind her, placing it into the small of her back. Immediately, he sensed her relax. In the last few weeks, her body language had changed. She wanted his protection, his presence, more than ever. They'd never spoken of it directly, but that was the thing when you'd been mated for so long: words weren't always required. He felt her need, and he wanted to provide for her.

She was his world.

And soon, a little mini vampire would come along and probably steal all their hearts.

Fuck, he really wanted it to be a male.

Having two females running around with a big piece of his heart might be more than he could take. He'd already had nightmares of his little princess falling in love with one of the male warriors and him *accidentally* beheading him. He'd even woken up grinning.

Yeah, that would just be a nightmare, alright.

Best it be a little male. Another little king.

In truth, he didn't know of any female Morettis being born in their bloodline. Kate, however, had not come to that realization yet, and when Brayden had nearly opened his big trap one day, he'd quickly shut it for him.

Vincent wasn't convinced they couldn't or didn't, more that it just hadn't happened, him being an expert in the matter.

So fine, he didn't actually know, but he was guessing. With such low breeding numbers, he genuinely believed it was possible.

The vehicles pulled in front of them, and members of *Operation Daylight* began to descend like they were in a movie premier of *Men in Black*. Secret service guys did their thing as, one by one, some of the most powerful humans on the planet walked into Vincent's castle.

His home.

Vincent could smell their fear, and so could every vampire around him. However, he respected their courage to be here, and saw it as a testament to the work they'd all done in building trust.

"James." He shook the president of the United States's hand. "Welcome. This is my mate, Kate Moretti."

"Kate. Lovely to see you. We met at the gala last year."

"Yes, I remember. Lovely to see you again," Kate greeted, accepting his handshake. "Please, say hello to Marie for me."

"I will. She sent Christmas wishes." James smiled.

Vincent had forgotten the charity gala they had attended; last year felt like an eternity ago, after all they had gone through since. He recalled Kate and the First Lady had gotten along very well, as she did with most people she met, which had included many of the First Ladies over the years.

One by one they greeted their guests, who were then directed by Seraphina into a nearby room they had set up for the cocktail hour.

Refreshments were handed out, and everyone made small talk. Vincent watched as nervous human eyes darted around the room. If they were expecting coffins and bats, they would be sorely disappointed. The human and Moretti security teams hovered around the periphery of the room, and he knew, the outside of the castle. He left that to the commander and prince to look after. The guests were his business.

Vincent led Kate to the front of the room after a time, and nodded at the prince. He and Willow made their way to stand beside them.

"Should've worn my tiara," Willow muttered.

"Tonight, sexy." Brayden grinned, patting her ass.

Vincent glared at them, and they smiled at each other. *Newly mated idiots.*

"Welcome to *Casa Moretti, Roma*," he said, his voice reaching all corners of the room. "I will admit, I never envisaged this day. I suspect my father and his father would be shocked to see so many humans standing within our walls."

Everyone bobbed their heads.

"However, this is an important day for us all. Trust is important, *essential*, in all relationships. We have much to share with you, and I suspect you will be rather bored with what you learn. There are no spooky bat caves…"

"Ah, that's Batman," Brayden muttered.

He ignored the prince. "…or sparkly vampires here."

A few sniggers broke out.

"Tonight, we have opened our home to you so we can break down the superstitions and horror born from Hollywood about our race, to build a solid platform where we can safely, without worldwide panic and hysteria, become visible to humans."

Cue the murmurs of agreement and nodding heads.

"I've said this to you all before, and I will say it again. We have lived among you since forever. We pose no harm. And just like you, we wish to live our lives, love our families, and thrive."

He held, for a moment, the eyes of the most notable members in the room.

There was no need to remind them they were surrounded by predators. Deep within their human nature was the animalistic knowledge of who was the deadliest. And it was that which made Vincent the most nervous. Humans were physically inferior to vampires. It was his job to make sure none of them felt threatened so they didn't take any actions that would harm his race.

Time was something not on his side. Time would allow humans to plan and organize to eradicate them, unless he was smart and made this work. He had to. All they wanted was, as he'd said, to continue living in harmony will all the species on this planet. Now that some humans knew about them, it was going to be a complex and long journey to ensure his race could do that.

Or war.

And he really fucking didn't want that. Not with his child coming into the world.

"I've introduced you to my mate, Kate. Now, let me introduce you to the prince, Brayden Moretti, and his mate, Willow. Our first princess. Although"—he glanced at Kate's bump—"there could be another one very soon."

Short polite laughs filled the room.

None of these men gave a shit about his unborn child, this wasn't a baby shower, but Vincent was nothing if not a strategist. He wanted them to see they were a family, with partners and brothers and babies. Just like them.

"Brayden is captain of the Royal Army and will be leading your tour today."

Heads nodded as he watched them take in the enormous vampire beside him. At six foot four, Brayden was the biggest vampire in the race. Craig was an inch shorter and slightly broader, but there was no doubting Brayden's one hundred percent alpha status.

That, and he held within him the Moretti blood.

"Welcome to our humble abode." Brayden grinned.

Vincent wasn't fooled by the prince's charming approach. He could crush every single one of these humans with his bare hands on his own, but he was a Moretti, and it was his job, and in his blood, to protect their race.

"We've collaborated with your security teams to ensure your safe arrival, but now that you are within the walls of the castle, there is limited access. I can appreciate how uncomfortable that may be for some of you, but you have both the king's and my assurances that your safety is a priority for us."

Vincent nodded to his guests to emphasize the prince's point because he was right. Anything less than their safe departure from the property would be unacceptable.

"Please follow my team's instructions and directions, and stay on the tour trail. You don't want to"—he cleared his throat—"bump into a wandering vampire."

Vincent's eyes darted to Craig, who was rubbing his cheek, doing a crap job at hiding his smirk.

Goddamn idiots. They were trying to scare the fucking humans.

"Stick to the tour and everything will be…dandy."

"And you won't get lost. This place is huge!" Willow interjected, grinning, and received a few sniggers for her efforts.

Thank you, Willow. Words he never thought he'd think.

"The princess is right; this is a large property," Vincent said, moving to wrap up the speeches. "We'll finish the tour with a grand dinner and have you back in your hotels by two in the morning. Let's begin, shall we?"

He clapped his hands together and people began to shuffle about. He shot Brayden a *what* look, and received a *what* look in return.

With a hand in the small of Kate's back, he led her toward the entrance.

The guests were being handed flyers and split into separate groups. One by one, they headed out and began their tour.

Willow seemed to be thriving in her princess role, chatting with some of the most powerful people on Earth. Brayden would be keeping an eye on her despite the fact she was now a vampire. No male liked their mate being close to other men, regardless of how insane their logic was.

Kate leaned into him, and he pressed his hand into her back.

They were keeping things simple tonight. They'd view the primary areas of the castle, including the living areas, the kitchen, and their training areas. The entire purpose was to show them vampires were just as normal as humans, who ate, slept, watched crap TV, and lifted weights—albeit much fucking heavier and reinforced—just like they did.

Hell, they even took a crap, just like humans. That was not in the tour.

At the end, they would show them a twenty-minute video on the history of the Moretti family, (some of) their properties and assets, the structure of the Royal Army, and the rebellion. Vincent couldn't be with all the teams, but he would be on hand for the video presentation and questions afterward.

Vincent moved Kate into his arms and kissed her forehead. "Let's get you back to the royal wing."

"Brianna is going to stay with the queen," Craig informed him, stepping over to them and tilting his head toward the crowd. "Willow wanted to do the princess thing."

Vincent glanced at Kate once more, and she nodded at him. Her easy agreement to the babysitting arrangement spoke volumes. One look at Craig and his intense stare at the queen told him the big guy was also concerned. They locked eyes and no words were required. They were both on high alert.

"I'm here!" came the bright voice of the redhead. "Come on, mama. I'm taking you up to rest. Hi and bye, sexy vampire."

Craig scooped his mate around the waist and planted a kiss on her lips. "Take care of the queen."

"I will," Brianna replied, patting the big guy's pecs.

Those two needed a permanent room.

"I want to know immediately if something happens, understand?" Vincent softly told the queen. She nodded and lifted her head for his kiss, which he delivered. Then Vincent watched as the two females slipped out the rear door.

"Bri will let us know if anything happens," Craig reassured him, reading his mind. "Immediately. For now, let's get this over with."

"Thank you," Vincent said, slapping the big vampire on the back and leading them out of the room.

Any moment now, he would be a father.
Fucking hell.

CHAPTER ELEVEN

England, 1891

Kate sat on the Victorian sofa in her room and stared at the wall. The same wall she'd been staring at for the past thirty minutes. Perhaps longer.

"I think you should try drinking something," Riccardo said, again.

Her eyes moved to his then down to the glass of plasma. The mineral-rich drink was a luxury few vampires enjoyed. Here, in the Moretti castle, it was in abundance. Mere blood was rarely seen. It wasn't that she came from a poor family…oh God. *Family*.

Her family was dead. Her parents killed. Their carriage had been stopped by thieves in the night and their necks sliced. They had been found inside the carriage, their bodies intact, not turned to ash, saved from exposure to the sun by the windowless vehicle.

Kate's eyes darted to Riccardo.

Shouldn't she be crying? Instead, she just sat there. Staring.

"They are at home? Their bodies."

"Yes." Riccardo nodded.

She nodded.

"Kate, please. You are in shock. Please drink."

She raised the glass and found her hand was shaking. Riccardo moved across the space and lifted it to her lips, his hand on the back of her head as she took a small sip. The warm liquid slid down her throat, and she swallowed. It sank into her stomach like a lump of wet concrete.

Kate's lips began to quiver.

"Wh-wh-who would do this?" she asked. "Why? Who, why? I don't understand."

"I don't know, but I will do everything I can to find out," Riccardo promised. "I don't want you to worry about anything. I will take care of you, Kate."

Tears began pouring down her face.

She didn't want him to take care of her. She wanted…a different male.

"Come." He wrapped his arms around her, and she fell against his chest. "It's going to be okay. Cry as much as you need. I'm here."

As Riccardo ran his hand up and down her back, Kate let herself receive his comfort. She had known him much of her life. As she'd told the king, both their families had been hoping they would mate, and they had joked about it in their younger years, but it had never happened.

Kate didn't believe him to be her mate. She had never felt anything except friendship for the male. Close friendship, yes, but never an ounce of attraction.

Now, with her parents tragically gone and the king making it very clear what he wanted from her, she had to make some decisions for her future. Kate would not shame her family name by becoming Vincent's lover. If he didn't believe her to be his mate, then obviously she was wrong.

She hated how her body craved his touch even as he rejected any idea of her being more than someone who could pleasure his cock, but the way his blazing eyes held hers, the way he'd growled like a bear when Riccardo had pulled her into his arms, made it difficult to give up all hope.

And yet, he had stormed out of the room without looking back at her, instructing Brayden to find out who had killed her parents. And she'd not seen him since.

Kate awoke to a sharp knock at the door.

"Come in," Riccardo indicated.

Her eyes blinked, clearing from her sleep, and she heard the door open. She became aware she was wrapped in a blanket, her head on Riccardo's knees. His hand lay across her waist, just under her breasts.

"Mr. Bocci, we need to ask you some questions," Brayden said. "Do you mind coming with us?"

Kate sat up, and the memories came flooding back.

Oh God. Mama, Papa. No.

Vincent and Brayden stood in the doorway of her room staring at the two of them. Her eyes met Vincent's. His brows were bunched together angrily, and his eyes were burning with an emotion she didn't fully understand.

"Of course. Any help I can be." He stood and looked down at Kate. "Will you—"

Vincent marched toward them, radiating authority and

power. "I'll take it from here, thank you, Mr. Bocci. Go with the prince, please."

Riccardo's eyes widened, then narrowed slightly as he turned back to her. "Yes, Your Majesty," he replied, patting Kate on the thigh, promising to return. Vincent's eyes didn't leave her face until the door closed behind the two vampires.

"I'm sorry for your loss," he said, his eyes softening. "Is there anything you need?"

She shook her head and began to fold the blanket.

"Kate?"

"I'm fine," she answered as tears began to flow down her face.

At this point, she had no control of her emotions. She was feeling everything. Shock. Grief. Anger. Fear for her future. Confusion.

Vincent sped across the distance and lifted her into his arms.

As soon as his body wrapped around hers and she felt the warmth of his embrace, she felt his strength comfort her. Suddenly, she began to shake and sob against his chest. With his powerful arms wrapped tightly around her, holding her head, she finally felt safe.

Cared for. Protected.

This was where she belonged; she knew it with every inch of her being.

But did he realize it yet?

Vincent lifted Kate into his arms and sat in the big armchair, tucking her against him. Finally, he would be able to comfort her. It had taken all his strength not to rip

Riccardo's limbs from his body when he'd pulled Kate into his arms upon delivering the tragic news. She had gone to him, and as a close family friend, Vincent had been powerless to berate either of them.

But he couldn't just sit there and watch, so he'd done what he could and instructed his team to help uncover what had happened to her parents. A challenging task, given Rome was over a thousand miles away.

But now Kate was in his arms, and he strangely felt like he was exactly where he should be. Slowly, her tears began to subside, and she lay resting against his chest. His thumb methodically rubbed her hip, and his heartbeat matched hers.

Vincent had held her in his arms a few times now, but this was the first time his cock had not been invited to the party. It was an intimate moment, despite the tragedy which brought them closer. She had lost her parents, and he had lost two vampires. Every vampire belonged to him, but he had also known Mr. and Mrs. Valentino.

He ran his hand up and down her back. "The sun will soon rise. Can I get you something to eat before you slumber?"

"No," she said quietly. "Perhaps I will try some more plasma in a little while."

Vincent glanced at the glass on the table in front of them and frowned. Riccardo had already thought of everything. Goddamn it. He wanted to be the male taking care of her. He should have come to her earlier.

"Let me get you a fresh glass," Vincent offered, moving to stand, but Kate dug her fingers into his arm, halting him.

"Please. Can we stay here a little while longer?"

"Yes," he replied, his voice gravel, relaxing back into

the seat. He wished he could stay there holding her forever, which was confusing as fuck.

"Will you stay with me today?" the little voice asked.

Vincent squeezed his eyes shut.

He had so many damn questions. Why did he feel like this about this particular female?

Kate was beautiful, vulnerable, strong.

And not his.

This felt like stolen time before their worlds split apart.

Soon, Riccardo, the male she'd told him her family had identified as her mate, would return. Was the male her mate? If he was, it would be completely wrong for him—king or not—to be holding her in his arms.

Did he give a fuck?

Absolutely not.

But he knew what would happen if he spent the day with Kate. It would include his currently inactive cock, and that would be going too far. As king, he was responsible for upholding the mating laws of the race.

Part of him was furious Kate had not mentioned the male and her potential mating to him before now. How could she have been pursuing him as her mate when she knew there was a male back home waiting for her.

He'd been on his way to confront her about it when they had heard the news about her parents.

"It wouldn't be appropriate, Kate. You know this."

She sat up, round, wet eyes staring at him astonished. "Because you are the king?"

"Because Riccardo is—might be your mate," he replied, his anger simmering beneath the surface. "I shouldn't even be here, Kate. If he…"

Her mouth fell open and she moved off his lap, wiping

her eyes.

The desire to stop her was strong, but he had to let her go. Vincent clenched the arms of the chair and glanced away.

"Then you should go," Kate ordered, her voice thick.

Vincent nodded. And didn't move.

He should leave. He should stand up and walk out of here, leaving her to grieve for the loss of her parents. Yet, he sat gripping the chair like he was hanging over the edge of a cliff.

He hated himself for wanting another male's mate. There had been no formal bonding, but he could see how close the two were, and it was wrong of him to interfere. It could be only a matter of time before they became bonded. So why did he want to beat the other male to a pulp?

Only Brayden ranting away telepathically had stopped him.

Suddenly, his eyes darted to Kate's. He wanted fucking answers.

"Why did you come to court, Kate?" he asked gruffly.

She wrapped her arms around her middle and slowly shook her head. "Just stop, please."

"Do you love him?" he continued, his voice a growl

"Yes," she answered. "But not—"

Vincent was on his feet before she could finish, anger pouring through his veins, startling her.

"Enough. I am sorry about your parents, but you should have stayed home with your mate and not…not have been…here."

Visions of their time together flashed between them. The glances. The kisses. How she had pleasured herself. His mouth on her breast.

How could she? How could any of it had taken place if she was meant to be with Riccardo?

Before he punched a hole in the wall, he marched across the room. As he reached the door, he heard her soft voice.

"Vincent." He froze, not turning. "You are a foolish male."

Clearly.

Feeling like an asshole, he pulled open the door and let it close loudly behind him. Kate's anguished cry ripped through his body, tearing his soul apart. He sped through the hall, teleporting to his room, and let out a scream which vibrated throughout the walls of the castle.

CHAPTER TWELVE

England, 1891

Kate stood beside the carriage as her bags were loaded, the gravel beneath her feet cold and harsh. Her breath was visible in the early night air as she took in the stars in the inky sky beginning to appear.

It had been a long day tossing and turning as she tried to sleep after Vincent had left. Her heart felt like it had been torn out of her chest and stomped on. In the past twenty-four hours, she had lost her parents and the male she thought was her mate. All she wanted to do was curl up in a ball and cry for about one hundred years.

When Riccardo had returned, Kate had agreed to return to Rome with him as soon as night fell. She wanted the comfort of her own home to grieve in and needed to arrange her parents' vigil. Plus, it was now clear she was not wanted at *Casa Moretti*. At least not by the king.

Kate felt embarrassed to have ever believed she was

his mate. No mated or bonded male would be able to watch another male embrace his female, especially not one as powerful as Vincent. He was a true alpha. Not once had he reacted as she'd seen other mating males do. If anything, he was just disgusted at her for her willingness to bed him when she had a potential mate at home. Had he let her speak, the stubborn male would have learned Riccardo was nothing but a friend.

The pain of his rejection was nearly as powerful as the pain from the loss of her parents. Together, she simply felt weak with grief and sadness.

Kate had spent all day reflecting on the time they'd spent together. Never had she dreamed of feeling such a connection with the king, or any male. Attending his coronation was something Kate had never expected—nor had any of them—when she'd decided to join her parents at court this season. She'd needed a break from life in Rome and the pressure of mating with Riccardo. They all knew it wasn't something one could force, so when they had invited Kate to join them in England, she had jumped on the opportunity.

Riccardo would be working at his father's firm, busy for the summer, so Kate had been excited about the time away to just relax and have fun. Her family and Riccardo's had been convincing them both for decades that they were made for each other. They were simply waiting for it to happen.

But it never had.

Kate understood her mama wanted grandbabies, but the distance from Riccardo had brought her much needed clarity. He wasn't, and never would be, her mate. Before her parents had left, she had spoken to her father and shared her thoughts. She was to stay on at court a little longer to decide if she would return home or travel to other parts of Europe, staying with family friends. She'd had her eye on Paris, and even Spain.

In truth, she had been hoping Vincent would be her mate and that they would return to Rome and announce the news.

Instead, her life had simply fallen apart.

Now she could only think ahead from one moment to the next.

When she'd met Vincent just mere months earlier, he'd still been a prince. While Brayden was infamous for his playboy lifestyle, Vincent was more serious. She had liked the way he held his tall frame, so confident, self-assured, and comfortable in his own skin. He had thinking eyes, as if thoughts and ideas were constantly fighting for dominance in his mind.

Kate had watched him exhibit kindness to those around him, despite being heir to the throne. This wasn't always the case in royal families. He had a strong relationship with his brother, evident by their open teasing of each other and their playfulness. She'd seen the love both boys had for the queen, their mother, and it went without saying they respected their father, the all-powerful king.

She had felt deeply for him after they had passed. It was why she had gone to him that day, to provide comfort and companionship. Without thinking, she'd knocked on his door, and he'd let her in. In more ways than one. Vincent had opened up in a way she doubted he did with many others, and Kate had felt closer to him than ever. Until he'd been clear with her about his priorities.

He wanted to fuck her. But the throne came first, and it always would.

Why, then, did his eyes talk to her and say something

different?

Clearly, she was in denial.

Kate had mistaken his lust for something else. There was nothing more to it.

Her lips pursed as she saw Riccardo walk out of the castle doors alongside Brayden and Craig. They all shook hands, and he began to walk toward the carriage.

Kate's eyes dropped.

She had known Riccardo for a long time, yet, for all his caring and kindness, there was a possessiveness about him she felt uneasy with. He had been more and more domineering over the past few years , even going so far as to make plans with her father, who had been successful in holding back the more dominant vampire, saying only that when they mated, Kate could decide. But it felt increasingly like the decisions were being taken away from her.

Now her father was dead.

Now Kate was leaving England to return home with Riccardo.

"Come, Katherine." And God, she hated when he called her by her full name. "Let's get you home where you belong."

As he placed his hand in the small of her back then took hold of her hips, lifting her into the carriage, Kate felt a cold shiver run through her. She tucked her black gown around her legs and removed her hat.

"Hey," Riccardo said, touching her cheek. "Everything will be okay. I promise to look after you."

She shook her head. "I don't need you to look after me, Riccardo."

He pressed his lips together. "I think we both know that's not true."

She stared at him and pursed her lips.

"Be good, Kate, please." He huffed.

She watched him climb inside and sit opposite her. Riccardo was a good-looking vampire. Tall, strong, though not in the way the warriors here at the royal household were, with wavy brown hair and green eyes. He turned those eyes on her again, and they flashed with want.

She looked away, not wanting to give him any wrong impressions.

Kate moved the curtain and glanced out at the Moretti castle one last time. Brayden gave her a nod and she returned it with a small smile before letting the heavy fabric drop as the horses began to move.

Her heart clenched painfully. Vincent hadn't come to say farewell.

She knew she'd been waiting for him, but hadn't wanted to admit it to herself.

She closed her eyes.

It was over.

His absence had told her everything she needed to know.

Kate pretended to sleep for most of the night while the carriage bounced its way back to Rome. They had crossed the channel between England and France the night before, and now, all she wanted was to be home.

Riccardo had updated her on stories from home, finally picking up his book when it was clear she wasn't interested in conversation. He'd said he understood she was grieving and would excuse her rudeness.

The longer she spent with him, the more irritated she

became.

In truth, her mood was darkening with anger at Vincent. With all this time on her hands, she kept reflecting back on their time together. The little moments, the glances, the touches, the winks.

Yes, Vincent Moretti had actually winked at her. How could she have been so foolish?

He was no charmer like Brayden Moretti—that vampire made no secret of his naughty ways, nor did any of his entourage. They winked at every luscious-looking vampire they came across. Vincent didn't, but he had winked at her. And she'd fallen for it.

Just because a vampire didn't play often, it didn't mean they didn't play sometimes.

Clearly, she was his *sometimes* plaything.

He hadn't lied though. He'd told her straight to her face he wanted to fuck her and keep her as his. Not as his mate.

God, she'd been so stupid.

He wanted her for his own entertainment, and he obviously didn't like sharing.

At the royal ball, the prince had asked her to dance, and Vincent had swooped in and pushed his brother aside. Her entire world had lit up when he'd placed his arm around her and led her to the dance floor. She'd felt like a princess in her emerald-green dress, the lace-trimmed bodice showing off her ample breasts which had caught the not-yet-king's eye. When the waltz had begun, Vincent had expertly led her around the dance floor.

When his eyes had met hers, her body had flared to life. The touch of his fingers had been like fire, flooding her sex with a heat and need she knew Vincent could see in her flushed face. He had pulled her body closer, his knee going deeper between her thighs as they danced, oblivious to those around them. Her body had been tingling with arousal by the end of the dance.

When he'd walked her off the dance floor, Kate had been ready for his whisper of invitation. Instead, he'd returned her to her parents' side and kissed her hand. The only whisper she had received was a thick, gravelly thank you.

His lingering gaze, though only for a moment, had told her more.

It had said *I want you, but I won't.*

If only she had listened. Now, her heart was aching as she sped toward Italy while Vincent sat in his castle making plans to move across the world to America. Preparing to meet his mate, crown his queen, and leaving Kate simply as a passing thought.

A tear slid down her face.

She would never see Vincent again.

And he hadn't cared enough to even say goodbye.

CHAPTER THIRTEEN

England, 1891

Vincent stood in the shadows of the library watching Kate as she stood by the carriage outside the front of his castle. He could see enough from where he stood to see the anguish on her face.

She was grieving.

He ached to go to her and pull her into his arms, but she already had a male to care for her. A male she fucking loved.

Damn her.

His fists and jaw clenched. He was furious she had never told him about Riccardo. Vincent wasn't a bloodthirsty vampire, but God, he wanted to kill the damn vampire, even if the male had done nothing wrong. He thought Kate to be his mate, and by the sounds of it, the two were fated. Vincent could never punish a vampire unfairly; he wasn't that kind of king, and never would be.

Not even for a female he lo—

No.

Vincent stopped his mind, pressing his fingers against his forehead.

She wasn't his.

He had no idea what game Kate had been playing at, but their time together, whatever it had been, was over.

He watched Riccardo shake Brayden's hand and walk toward Kate. When he placed his hands on her, helping her into the carriage, Vincent gripped the window ledge and snapped it off the wall.

Fuck.

He tossed it across the room and let out a growl.

Just before the vehicle departed, he saw the fabric move and her longing look.

That's when he knew she was looking for him. He had disappointed her.

Same, sweetheart.

Vincent was full of fury, regret, and disappointment.

"I know I've been in denial about my feelings for you, Kate," he told her through the glass. "But I was beginning to think you *were* mine."

It was true. He'd begun to wonder if she could be his fucking queen, until she had said she loved another male.

Now he knew she wasn't.

He watched as the carriage began to move, then turned and walked away.

CHAPTER FOURTEEN

Present Time

Brianna placed the bowl of popcorn under her nose, and Kate shook her head.

"Sofi?" Bri asked, passing it the other way.

"*Grazie*," Sofia said, taking a handful of the salty snack.

The three of them were sitting on her bed, leaning up against the enormous headboard watching Netflix. *Bridgerton*, to be exact.

"You know, I'm kind of jealous you guys lived during this period. The dresses are gorgeous," Bri sighed.

Kate snorted.

"They weren't that bright and colorful in real life. Nor did we have the modern plumbing for regular bathing we have now. Trust me, toilets back then, and those dresses…just no."

Sofia nodded knowingly while Brianna screwed her nose up.

Kate ran her hand over her belly. The baby was less active, a sign she'd been told meant labor was close. She knew it would be soon, but whether that was minutes, hours, or days, she wasn't sure. She was hoping their little vamp would wait at least a few more hours.

"Didn't you meet Vincent in the eighteen hundreds?" Bri asked.

"Yes. In England." She nodded, remembering back to the most difficult and beautiful time in her life. "The king took his time realizing he was my mate, though, but we eventually got together. Obviously."

"Did he woo you? Like all *Sense and Sensibility?* Mr. Darcy? It must have been sooooo romantic in those days," Brianna gushed, all but swooning as she sat on the bed next to her.

"No." Kate snorted. "Honestly, you females need to stop watching this romantic fiction nonsense. No male can live up to it."

"You're not wrong." Sofia laughed. "Life was not as glamorous back then as the TV shows make them out to be. The men were definitely not gentlemen, even if they dressed the part."

They shared a knowing glance.

"Nope. I love it," Brianna said stubbornly. Kate wasn't surprised. Bri was a terrible romantic, and Kate wondered for the millionth time how on earth Craig had won the female's heart. Clearly, he was a big teddy bear behind closed door.

Kate grinned to herself. *No damn way.* He probably had a magic cock.

"Come on, you're no pushover, Kate. How did Vincent win your heart?"

It was strange thinking back to that time. Most of the

people in the royal household had been around when they had been courting, for want of a better word, and were reasonably familiar with what had taken place. It had been a painful time, losing her parents and waiting for Vincent to realize he loved her and finally accept she was his mate.

"He did it in his own way," she answered. "And most definitely in his own time."

And just in time.

Sofia turned and tucked her feet underneath her. "I heard he nearly lost you. Is that true?"

Kate nearly gave her automated answer. Vincent was the king, and their life was private, but these females were family. Even if Sofia was a new addition, they had grown close, and she valued their friendship. Plus, she was feeling very emotional and hormonal with this bundle of arms and legs inside her.

Vincent's child.

Once upon a time, Kate had thought she would never see him again, let alone be carrying his child. The heir to the Moretti throne.

She shook her head.

"Yes, and I nearly lost him," she said, traces of the sadness from long ago creeping into her voice. "It was a terrible time. Vincent had just taken the throne after losing his parents, and a male who fancied himself my mate showed up to tell me mine had been tragically killed."

Brianna gasped. "Oh, God. I'm so sorry. I never wondered where your parents were. Is that bad?"

Kate smiled at the female and patted her leg.

"No. You've had a lot of changes and sadness in your own life, Brianna. This happened a long time ago. You are always caring about others."

Brianna chewed on her lip, and Kate knew she'd be

kicking herself for days over it. There was nothing anyone could do or say. People processed things in their own way. She smiled at her again, and Brianna nodded. "Okay. Still, I'm sorry."

"So what happened?" Sofia asked. "Did Vincent beat the bad guy up and save the girl?"

"Huh! These movies are getting to you, too." Brianna laughed.

Sofia giggled.

"No, I'm just mated to an alpha male and have seen them all in action. Namely your Craig. My God, that male is intimidating when another male comes near you."

"I know. It's so hot." Brianna grinned.

Kate laughed. They were all familiar with Craig's growls and snarls around his mate. He was very close to his inner predator, and it was why he was the commander of their army.

"Here." Kate reached over and grabbed the framed photo from her bedside cabinet. It was small. A surprise gift from the king, as color photography was very new in the 1890s and a great luxury. She remembered the day. It had been her birthday, and her first without her parents. They were due to leave for America the next day. An emotional moment, but it was, looking back, the start of her new life. A happier life. One she had thought would never happen.

She handed Brianna the photograph.

"This was several months after we mated, in England. Your king *did* finally realize I was his mate, but just in the nick of time, as they say in your movies."

"Holy shit. Vincent has teeth. Did you know he had teeth? He's smiling," Brianna teased. "But seriously, all jokes aside, he looks so happy."

"Oh, girl, I know he has teeth, trust me." Kate laughed.

"TMI, TMI," Brianna said, holding out her palm. "God, it's like hearing my parents talk about sex. Nope, nope, nope."

Kate burst out laughing.

She took the photo back and looked at it again. While they all looked around the same age—because vampires—Brianna wasn't wrong; Vincent did look happy. They had both found their happily ever after.

Eventually.

"Okay, ladies, you need to help me get this damn gown on. We need to glam up for this dinner."

"Only if I can try on your crown," Bri said, jumping off the bed.

Nope.

Nobody wore her crown. She had worked way too hard to win the heart of her king to share it for even a second.

Sofia sent her a knowing smile. Kate winked at her. There was something about the female. It was as if her suffering had made her incredibly intuitive. She just seemed to sense things without words needing to be spoken. Kate liked that about her very much.

As the two females helped her get off the bed, Kate focused back on the present time. God, she was looking forward to getting this baby vamp out of her.

And becoming a mother at last.

CHAPTER FIFTEEN

Present Time

"So you left England in 1901 and settled in Maine," James Adler said. "And you built a damn castle without anyone knowing?"

Vincent heard Craig and Lance snort and shot them a look.

"It was nearly finished by the time we arrived in the United States, but the world was a different place back then, James. No Google Maps, fewer people around to see what was going on, and a greater trust," Vincent answered.

The president's question was a good one; however, Vincent wasn't going to answer truthfully, and he had zero guilt about it. They'd been able to survive unexposed as a race with one important tool: their ability to manipulate human minds. They could wipe or rearrange memories as they required. If humans discovered they were able to do this, all bets were off. They would never be trusted.

Even among vampires, it was a tool rarely used. They were well aware of its power, so much so that parents took their role in teaching their children to use it very seriously. Any misuse of it soon had consequences. By the time they were young adults, vampires understood it was frowned upon to use it nefariously, and that it should only be used when necessary, such as when protecting the race's existence.

To remain hidden, there were times it was needed. For example, if your boss asked you to work a day shift, which was impossible for a vampire, then you simply entered their mind and insisted they select someone else; manipulate their thinking.

"Yeah, but still. A fucking castle. In the United States?" POTUS said, shaking his head. "And we never knew, and still don't know, it exists?"

Vincent held the man's stare. "Well, you do now."

This is where things got tricky. Their tech team worked twenty-four seven blocking satellites and cleaning up data records of their existence. He didn't want them knowing that either.

"Look, there are going to be things you are not going to like hearing as you learn more about us, but we have done—and will continue to do—what we need to do to survive and protect our race. It's nothing less than what any of you do every single day," Vincent finished, wiping his mouth on his napkin. He wasn't going to sugarcoat things.

Jeromy Smithers, the United Kingdom's prime minister, nodded. "He's right."

"If we're being honest, we would have done worse," Chung Lee, from South Korea, added.

"There's no denying you have lived peacefully alongside us for a very long time," Jeromy said. "The more I learn, the more I am beginning to understand, yet the more questions I have."

Vincent felt a rare smile begin to bubble up. Perhaps it was relief that his strategy was working. All he wanted was for his race to coexist with humans in peace. He knew there was a long journey ahead of them; still, he mentally patted himself on the back and enjoyed the moment. When you were at the top of the food chain, there was no one else to do it.

There was also no one else to blame if things turned to shit.

Yeah, it was lonely at the top. Thank God he had Kate. He never would have survived his reign if he'd lost his mate even before he knew she was his.

Seraphina glanced at him, and he nodded with his eyes.

"Gentlemen, it's time for dinner," Vincent announced, clapping his hands. "Please use the facilities to freshen up, and we will see you in thirty minutes."

Seraphina took the floor, giving their guests further instructions, and Vincent exited the room. He was eager to get back to Kate.

"Vince," Brayden said, walking alongside him. "Willow said Kate looks ready to pop. Are you sure she should join us tonight?"

He arched a brow. "Has something happened?"

"No. But do you really want her surrounded by humans if she goes into labor?" Brayden asked.

Vincent continued walking and pushed through two doors before he stopped. When they were out of earshot, he turned to his brother. Brayden's tone had caught his attention.

"What's your concern?" he asked, placing his hands on his hips.

"I just don't think it's wise. When she goes into labor, I know your diplomacy will fly out the window. Tell Kate to stay in the royal wing with one of the females, and we can be there in seconds if needed."

"No," he denied, continuing his walk. "If her waters break, we will simply deal. The queen needs to attend."

"Stop, Vincent. Your child is about to enter this world. The heir to the Moretti throne," Brayden growled at him.

Jesus.

Vincent ran a hand over his face.

"I'd just rather it didn't happen while some of the most important humans on the planet are present," Brayden continued.

The prince was doing his job. He wasn't as close to these humans as Vincent had been over recent months. The trust built between them had not extended to his brother, and it was something he hadn't considered. Brayden was in charge of security, and he lived and breathed it. Ensuring the queen and the newest heir were safe was on the top of his mind. Vincent appreciated his perspective, but having the queen bow out of such an important occasion was just not acceptable.

Kate also wouldn't want to stay behind. She knew the importance of these things, and while she wasn't thrilled about it, Vincent knew he would have a tough time convincing her and pay the price if he put his foot down.

Brayden had done his job as captain by raising it. The final decision was his, as king.

"Well, best you make sure your team is prepared for such an event. It's their job to protect the queen, so tell them to do their goddamn job. Enough, brother. Kate is attending."

They stared at each other for a moment and then Brayden walked off, shaking his head and dropping his favorite curse word.

CHAPTER SIXTEEN

Present Time

"Will you stop it." Sofia laughed as she slapped Lance on his solid and very sexy chest. "This is the third time I've redone my lipstick."

"Totally worth it," Lance said, pulling her toward his lips again.

It really was. She'd never tell him that, though. If she'd learned anything in the past few months living with all these alpha males, it was that if you gave an inch, they'd take a mile. Not that she minded Lance taking *all the miles* when it came to her body and the pleasure they shared.

"You look fucking gorgeous," he purred against her mouth. "If any of those humans even look sideways at you, I'll snuff them."

"Snuff them?"

"Yeah. You know, like the godfather." He grinned.

"I'm not sure that's…" Sofia started as her phone

began ringing. She wriggled, and Lance placed her back on her feet reluctantly.

"Better be important," he mumbled, turning back to the mirror to straighten his suit. They were getting ready for the dinner tonight, and Lance was looking so damn sexy she didn't want to leave the room.

Sofia lifted her phone and saw her brother's name.

"*Ciao*, Ben," she greeted, happy to hear from him. They had been separated for over seventy years, and she loved having him back in her life. Not that she had seen much of him since she'd moved into the castle.

In fact, Sofia had sent him multiple invitations to join them for a meal, much to the chagrin of her mate, and so far, Ben had declined every single one in his own cheeky way.

They had met for dinner in Rome, where Lance had paced the footpath nearby, even when she had assured him she was safe with her own brother. And not just because Ben was her brother.

Her *big* brother was, well, huge.

Ben looked as big as one of the senior lieutenants in King Moretti's army. He definitely hadn't looked like that seventy years ago. He'd never been a slim, small male, but now, his body was toned and powerful. Even Sofia could see that.

She'd overheard discussions between Lance and Craig. They were worried. She didn't understand why; it wasn't like they were the only strong vampires on Earth. One day, she had finally snapped and told them to stop being dramatic, reminding them there were gyms in America where he could have gotten into shape.

"*No, Sofia, there aren't,*" Craig had responded darkly. "*Not a warrior's body like that.*"

"*It's not just his body, Sofi. It's the way he holds himself. He's trained,*" Lance had added.

"*By fucking who, though?*" Craig had asked as if she wasn't there.

She'd scoffed at them. "*Don't tar Ben with being the enemy just because I was. He left. Seventy years ago,*" she had reminded them. "*He's not part of the rebellion. It's why he fell out with my father and left in the first place.*"

"*That's the problem,*" Craig had growled. "*We don't think Ben is a member of the rebellion. But he's also not with us. That's the damn mystery.*"

Sofia had shaken her head and left them to their conspiracy theories.

She was just grateful to have Ben back in her life, especially after discovering her parents had been responsible for brainwashing her her entire life about the rebellion and had single-handedly sold her to the leader who had kidnapped her then attempted to rape her. Again.

Having a family member she trusted was important to Sofia, and she really wanted to believe she could trust him. She wasn't being naive, but Ben had done nothing to show he was untrustworthy. In any case, it was her mate's job to worry about the king's safety, so she couldn't blame him, but it didn't mean he was right.

"*Hey, babycakes, how's it going?*"

Sofia rolled her eyes and grinned at the very American greeting. He'd been away from Italy for far too long.

"It's going good, thank you. We're about to head to an event. Is everything okay?" she asked.

"*For sure. I was just wondering if the invite to visit was still open?*" Ben asked, and she could nearly see the dimples that would be on display by the cheeky tone in his voice.

Her face lit up.

Sofia poked her tongue out at Lance when he shook his head at her, his vampire hearing giving him full access to her private phone call.

"*Sì,* yes, when?" she asked eagerly.

"*How's tomorrow? I could pop by late evening.*"

"Lovely. Great. Around ten?"

She was working but would be finished around that time and be able to spend a few hours with him. The thought of him coming to see her new home filled her heart. Their dinner had been short, and with Lance pacing outside, Sofia had been stressed. His twenty-five texts hadn't helped. Having Ben at the castle meant Lance could relax knowing she was safe inside the walls. In theory.

The look on his face was making her wonder if her theory was a little off.

"*Perfect. I can't wait to see where you live, Sofi. I hear it's pretty big.*" Ben laughed.

"Yes, you should see the mortgage I have on this place." She grinned. Lance rolled his eyes, and she turned away, ignoring him. It was so fun to be joking around with her brother again. As kids, they had been close, but over time, they had grown apart.

She now understood why. Their father. Obviously, when Ben had shown signs of disagreeing with the rebellion, he had kept them apart.

Now they were free to reconnect and get to know one another again.

Ben laughed. "*See you tomorrow.*"

Sofia put her phone down on the bed and turned to face the music.

"You're not meeting with him alone," Lance said, not missing a beat.

"Yes. I am," she replied, crossing her arms. "If you ever want to have sex again."

Lance raised his eyebrows at her.

"Seriously, what do you think is going to happen? He has to go through security—*your* security—and then he'll be surrounded by Moretti soldiers. He's my goddamn brother." She shook her head. "You are being ridiculous."

Lance let out a long sigh.

"You know what, do what you want. You'll just watch us on the cameras or from the shadows anyway," she sighed back at him.

Lance took her face in his hands. "Because I love you. It's my job to protect you, and nothing you say will stop me from doing that. God, Sofia, if anything happened to you…"

She glanced down.

After what they had been through, what she had endured, she knew Lance was overly protective, even for a mated vampire.

"I know. But he's my brother, Lance." She looked back at him, need in her eyes. "I need my family, and he's all I have."

"Fuck," he cursed, dropping his forehead to hers. They stood like that for a little while before he lifted his head and sighed again. "I'll have to brief the team, and then it's up to Craig to decide what happens from a security standpoint. That's not my call. But I will give you some space with your brother if it's within my power to do so."

Neither of them had any control over that, Lance was right.

Sofia nodded and whispered *thank you*.

She knew Craig would make sure her brother was well

aware he was being watched.
	And intimidated.

CHAPTER SEVENTEEN

Present Time

Kate held Vincent's arm as the security guards pulled open the double doors to the large dining room. She could see the large candles filling the room with warm light and the long cream drapes around the windows, drawn to create an intimate and friendly space, as she'd asked.

Vincent glanced down at her, and she smiled. "I'm fine."

"Immediately, Kate. As soon as you feel a contraction, you tell me, and I am getting you out of there."

She rolled her eyes. "Yes. Fine. I promise. You have told me that several times in the past ten minutes."

He grunted.

Ahead of them, Brayden stood with Willow on his arm. The princess was wearing a gorgeous lilac mermaid-style gown. Kate had loaned her a diamond choker, and every time Willow touched it, it brought a smile to her lips.

Kate remembered the night Vincent had gifted it to her, out in the rose garden. It had been the nineteen nineties.

Springtime.

The sky had been lit up by a full moon and sprinkled with stars. Kate had organized a picnic meal for them outside. She'd had no idea he was going to present her with such a beautiful gift. She'd had no idea he even remembered the date.

The day he had come to her and claimed her as his mate.

Outside, under the stars, he had kneeled and opened the long velvet box. Tears had sprung to her eyes and her hand had flown to her mouth. (Brianna would have been proud of her very Victorian response.) She'd truly been awestruck at her mate honoring that important day in their lives, one hundred years later.

"*Thank God I figured it out*," was all he'd said, in true Vincent fashion.

Kate had let the tears flow when he'd put it around her neck, and she'd done the fingering thing just as Willow was doing now. Vincent had pulled her into his arms and whispered in her ear, "*Because I couldn't have survived without you, my darling.*"

No one could ever understand how important these little moment with her mate were.

Vincent had spotted Willow wearing it before they'd left the room. He had glanced at her in question.

"*She's family. This is what queens do, my darling.*" Then she had glanced down at her enormous six carat diamond ring and smiled. The day he had come to claim her in 1891, Vincent had placed it on her hand, and the rest was history.

"*That does not leave your finger*," he had said this evening, planting a kiss on her lips as she murmured *never*.

Ahead of them, Willow and Brayden stepped inside the room filled with music, and they followed. The long table was dressed formally with a white tablecloth, crystal glasses, and silverware dating back centuries.

Kate took her seat first, followed by the king at the head of the table. Opposite her were the prince and princess, and sprinkled around the table were their guests, important members of the household, and their partners.

She leaned forward to take them all in, bumped her tummy, and groaned.

James Adler, who was sitting beside her, leaned back and gave her a smile. "We have three children."

"That's right. Vivienne, Samantha, and David."

"I'm impressed." He grinned.

"I'm a queen." She winked. "It's what we do."

James raised his glass in a mock toast, and they laughed.

Down the table, she spotted Tom and Lucinda, Lance and Sofia, Craig and Brianna. Kurt and Marcus had also joined them, unmated and both looking dapper. All of them were dressed in black evening suits, and the females wore beautiful rich-colored gowns and sparkling jewels. They didn't do this enough anymore, and Kate decided it would be a wonderful tradition to start doing it on a regular basis.

Starting with a Christmas meal.

Vincent would be thrilled.

She grinned to herself.

"So James, how did you enjoy the tour?" Kate inquired.

"Very enlightening. I'm not sure what I was expecting, but it's true, your lives are not dissimilar to a human's. It's still incredible we haven't known about you for so long," he said, shaking his head and glancing around the table. "But I do appreciate why you would fear exposing your race."

Kate nodded. She didn't want to expand on that during dinner.

They all knew why.

"Say, should you be here?" he asked, nodding at her belly.

"If you ask my mate, then no, but I am fine. Just pregnant." She laughed, forking salmon into her mouth.

Everyone made small talk as the meals were served and the wine flowed. Or water, in her case. It was polite and boring as all these types of events were.

"Moretti, I didn't realize you celebrated Christmas. Do you subscribe to the Christian faith, or…?" one of the humans further down the table asked loudly.

Willow choked on her truffle.

Brianna grinned into her glass of water.

Craig coughed out a *Christ, here we go*.

Kate dabbed at her mouth with her napkin, stifling a grin, and glanced at the king. Who was staring right at her.

"This is our first," she answered, as straight faced as she could. "We thought, with a baby on the way, it would be a nice touch."

Kate was not about to share that the two females across from her, and a few others further down, used to be human. Or how the males who had claimed them had taken a nice juicy bite of their neck (or whatever part of the anatomy they had chosen), and drained them of their blood before feeding them their own and turning them into fancy new vampires. And that they missed Christmas, so they were doing it for them.

Mostly.

I mean, she could…but it would put them off their Tiramisu. She also didn't think Vincent had covered that topic with them yet.

"It wasn't my choice," Vincent grumbled, waving his spoon at Brianna and Willow. "But we have a couple of Christmas elves among us who insisted."

"I mean, we can't take all the credit," Brianna started, smiling like she was on a toothpaste commercial. "Your idea of the little reindeer family was adorable," she added, stretching the last word out.

Vincent choked on his sip of wine and began coughing.

Kate leaned over, patting his back, and chewed her lip.

"Seriously, Brianna, you are going to get me killed." Craig muttered under his breath, shaking his head.

"Oh, we don't do that sort of thing." Bri nodded to the human opposite her. "My mate is joking."

"Right," Craig drawled, nodding and throwing back the remains of his wine.

"He just looks scary."

"Stop talking, Bri," Craig grunted under his breath.

Kate glanced at the king.

His raised brows and glistening eyes met hers. She could see he was torn between laughing and letting rip. She loved how the redhead gave her mate a run for his money. Vincent had never said anything, but she knew on some level he loved Brianna's spirit.

Kate sure did. It would be easy to mistake her playfulness for something else, but the former human was sharp as a knife. She had them all wrapped about her gorgeous little finger, but she knew where the boundaries were.

Kate could see the humans were enjoying the

humorous banter between them, and the fact it had relaxed them all enough to reflect the disjointed family they were was again a credit to the smart redhead.

She knew Vincent was smart enough to pick up on it too.

Kate glanced across at Willow, who was quieter than usual. She wondered how it felt for the females to be in the presence of such powerful leaders. These men would have been completely inaccessible to them several months ago. Now they were dining with them.

Willow smiled across at her, mouthing her question, asking if she was okay.

Kate nodded.

They were all concerned, knowing the baby was coming. She was hoping he or she would wait a few more days and be their little Christmas gift.

"So, Brianna, tell me about your role. What do you do here at the castle?" the UK prime minister asked.

"Well, I have quite a special role…" she began as Craig threw back more wine.

A few hours later, Vincent stood at the front door and watched the last of the vehicles drive off through the gates.

The females had taken Kate home as the meal finished, leaving him and the prince, along with Craig, other Moretti officials, and the SLCs, to stand around drinking brandy. Alcohol barely hit the sides of a vampire; they metabolized it too fast. Some could also drink fast and enjoy the buzz, but that wasn't what tonight had been about.

Vincent knew his team had been pacing themselves, if not nursing their drinks, to stay sharp and alert should the need arise. But as expected, the evening had gone smoothly.

All the world leaders had asked a wide range of questions and seemed, for the most part, comfortable.

But these were men practiced at playing a role, and Vincent wasn't going to be played for a fool. Not when it came to the safety of his race. *Operation Daylight* would continue to meet frequently, and he expected some interesting conversations when they met next in the new year.

"I'd like to see this prison of yours," James had requested quietly when the two of them had a private moment. Vincent wasn't surprised. The president and he had worked together to break up the laboratory where experiments were being performed on vampires, and he was privy to a few more things than the rest of the team.

"It only contains vampires. We do not concern ourselves with enforcing human laws," Vincent replied. "Although some of our kind *do* work in law enforcement."

"God, this really is going to take some getting used to," James said, shaking his head.

Vincent slapped him on the shoulder. "I get it. We've had thousands of years. And it's for that reason we ask you to continue to trust there are no nefarious intentions behind our existence."

James nodded and rubbed his forehead.

"It's going to be a damn difficult sell to most of the population, though, Vincent. Most don't trust their local senator, let alone a whole new species."

"Which is why we need to do our due diligence and have structures in place. With this fast-moving age of technology, we cannot continue to hide for much longer," he said, frowning. "Like we have reiterated here multiple times, it's in the interests of both humans and vampires to make sure we get this right."

James tossed back his brandy and stared into the now

empty crystal glass.

"Look, I think this event has achieved what we wanted." The president glanced around the room. "Everyone is on board and can see you all live a pretty normal, *humanlike* life. Now we need to expand. We need experts working with us on this."

Vincent laughed and took a drink.

"You have interspecies PR experts at the White House?"

"Consider it a new department," President Adler replied, laughing with him.

Vincent swirled his drink inside the cut crystal and nodded. "Yes. Okay. We are learning as we go. I'll arrange a private tour through our prison before you leave Italy. What I share with you remains between you and I for now."

"Jesus, what am I going to see down there?" James raised a brow.

Vincent shook his head. "Nothing. They are treated *humanely,* as you would call it. It's the punishment you won't like."

"Hey, we still have the death penalty in some states in the US," James said, waving a hand.

Vincent looked up and saw a few other humans walking toward them.

"I am a fair king, James. The vampires who end up in my prison are dangerous predators." He glanced up again. "Let's continue this discussion when you return."

"It will have to wait until after the holidays. My schedule is tight, as you can imagine."

They had been interrupted at that point.

He turned and walked back inside the foyer, hearing someone shut the doors behind him. Craig was leaning on the banister of the large staircase, and a few of the SLCs stood nearby. Brayden stepped up.

"I think that went well," the prince said.

"It was definitely good progress," Vincent agreed. "We have a long way to go, and hopefully, time to do so. Good work tonight, everyone. I need you to be extremely vigilant over the next few months and years."

They all nodded.

Not one vampire among them would risk anything.

"Ears and eyes to the ground, make sure our teams are well resourced, rested, and focused."

"Gotcha," Craig said.

"Tell Brianna I have a job for her." Vincent looked at Craig. "We need a PR and communications team. After all this Christmas...stuff, I want her and Willow to work with me to build this team. It is, after all, their background."

"I'll speak to Willow." Brayden nodded. "She'll be pleased to have something to focus on."

"Keep her out of trouble, you mean." Craig smirked.

"That too." He laughed.

"I'll set up a meeting," Vincent interrupted, beginning to make his way back home to Kate. "Tell them to enjoy the holidays. Work starts January 1st."

CHAPTER EIGHTEEN

Present Time

Sofia tapped the screen harder.

"Damn thing. It keeps locking up," she mumbled, clicking the power button on the side of her tablet. "Okay, let's forget that. How are things going today?"

Anna sat on the sofa opposite Sofia with her legs tucked under her. She looked like she should have been on a college campus in California or maybe Florida, with all that long curly hair and those brilliant blue eyes.

Beauty aside, you'd never know she'd suffered such trauma. At first glance.

While Anna's skin glowed with vampire youth, and her freshly styled hair looked carefree, when you looked closer, you could see the pain in the depths of her eyes. They were, after all, the windows to the soul.

Sofia knew because she could see it in her own reflection still, some days.

While she had the most amazing mate in Lance De Luca, who was patient, loving, protective, and the most understanding male any sufferer of sexual abuse could want, the path to healing was her own.

And it would be so for Anna. If she would begin to face what had happened.

God, she could understand why the pretty blonde wouldn't want to.

Sofia had witnessed the labs Anna had been held in. It had been one of the most gut-wrenching and terrifying moments of her life. Inside the cold, sterile room, vampires had been laid out on metal beds, conscious while being experimented on by humans. One had stared at her with pleading eyes, unable to move, speak, or help itself.

And she had been just as useless.

She had been undercover as a spy for the Moretti royal family when Stefano Russo had invited her to tour the facility. Had she attempted to free them, he would have simply overpowered her. So she had been left with only one choice: to act as if she were part of the rebellion still and go along with the tour.

Sofia had excused herself to go to the bathroom at one point and vomited.

Anna had been one of the thirty-seven vampires taken from their lives and experimented on in those labs. Now it was Sofia's job to help them. To guide them to a place where they could live and thrive once more.

"I'm good," Anna replied. "Oh, and before we get started, I fed the fish today, just in case someone else does it. I'm super worried they're going to get fat if we overfeed them, so we should create like a roster or something."

When they'd built the rehabilitation center, Sofia had insisted they bring in some pets. It was no secret they were wonderful for healing, so inside they had three goldfish, a very fluffy cat called Morris, a canary, and a hamster.

"Also, did you know that fish commit hurry curry?" Anna added.

"Hurry curry?" Sofia asked, pulling her brows together.

"Yes, you know..." Anna grinned, slicing her finger across her throat.

"Really?" Sofia's eyes widened. "I've never had fish."

"Well, it's not like they find a knife and slit their...you know. But apparently, they jump out of the fish tank," Anna explained, then her eyes darted around the room.

Sofia watched her. This was how their sessions went. Anna was now looking for another distraction. Another mindless topic to discuss.

Anything but talking about her experience.

"Sounds like the fish became intolerant of their life in a bowl," Sofia said.

Anna's eyes darted to hers. "*Sì*, perhaps."

"Have you spoken to your family this week?" Sofia asked, and Anna shook her head. "Did you want to invite them here for another visit?"

The families had visited a few times.

"No. *Mamma* is working long hours. *Papà*...well, he is struggling with what happened. You know..." Anna waved her hand in front of her. "I don't want to make it harder for them."

Sofia leaned forward an inch. "Where do you fall in all of this?"

Anna looked at her, bunching her forehead. "Me?"

"Yes. You, *cara*," Sofia confirmed, using the endearment because God knew the poor child deserved it. She was a darling. The sweetest little soul Sofia had met. She always worried about others, even in the face of what she had endured.

"Oh, no, I am fine. It's nice being here." Anna's eyes clouded over, then suddenly widened. "It's okay if I stay here a bit longer, isn't it?"

"*Sì*, Anna. For as long as you need." Sofia leaned back in her chair and tilted her head. "We discussed going for a wander around the castle. Are you still interested in doing that today?"

Anna immediately brightened. "Oh yes."

Sofia nodded, pleased with the response, though it wasn't necessarily a sign of progress. An opportunity to see inside one of the Moretti castles wasn't offered to very many vampires, so this was a big deal.

Sofia's job was to guide Anna in her healing journey. The fact she didn't want to go home was concerning. If Anna continued on this path of pleasing everyone else and not facing her own pain, she would never find a way out of her inner hell. If home wasn't a safe or nurturing place for her to heal, then it was right for Anna to stay at the rehabilitation center.

Sofia knew the king would never put an end date on their care.

She tapped the tablet, and it finally unfroze.

"Let me update my notes, and then we'll head out."

"Awesome! I'm going to change," Anna exclaimed, jumping up. "Are there any rules or a dress code?"

Sofia smirked. "No, but there are a lot of unmated warriors out there who need to remain focused on their job, so keep that in mind."

Anna blushed, smiled, and left to change.

Sofia's smirk faded.

She really hoped she could help this bright soul. When

they had first recovered them from the labs, Anna had been unconscious. It had taken them a few hours to bring her back. Initially, she'd gone into a state of shock, violently shaking like the others, but Anna's had worn off quickly. They had thought this was a good sign, but rather than talk about what had happened, Anna evaded any discussion about her experience.

The team had recognized it for what it was: avoidance.

It was a tactic often used by victims to avoid facing the reality of what had happened to them. Some even went so far as to make up an entirely different reality for themselves, which sounded fantastic; if only it were that easy. Unfortunately, it was surface level stuff. Underneath, in one's subconscious, the pain still existed, and the suffering remained. Just at a deeper level.

Initially, the team had let her be. If it helped Anna settle into her new surroundings and learn to trust them, they were okay with it. Except, while the others had begun to heal and make progress, Anna had kept her safety net in place.

Now it was time to stretch her.

If Anna wouldn't go home, a place where sufferers were often triggered, then venturing out into the castle was a good next option.

Sofia had organized a walk around the castle and planned to "bump" into Willow and Brianna, who would just so happen to be having dinner in the Great Hall. Her friendship with the two females had been blossoming since she'd mated Lance, but it was the relationship she had with the queen she valued most. Kate was an incredible female: inspirational, kind, and strong. They had both led a lonely life before meeting their males, and it had connected them.

Sofia texted Bri to let her know they'd meet them in about an hour.

Coolio, see you soon! the reply came, and she smiled.

Next, she messaged Ben, who was meeting her after she finished work today. She had no idea what to expect from the Moretti security when her brother showed up, and Lance had said nothing more other than to expect Craig to make his presence known.

Great.

Ben replied, ***see you at ten***, so Sofia slipped her phone into her back pocket and put her focus back on Anna.

This was important. She'd worry about the males in her life later.

Speaking of males, Sofia strongly suspected once the single males in the castle caught sight of Anna, there would be great interest. With her small frame, beach blonde waves, blue eyes which gave even the queen's stunning sapphires a run for her money, and perfect set of double Ds, there was no way she'd go unnoticed.

And there were some damn hot males roaming the halls of this castle. She may be a mated female, but she was not blind. Because that was the only way you'd miss all the abs, pecs, broad chests, sultry smirks, and solid thighs wherever you looked.

Not that they dared smirk at her.

Lance was a senior member of the Moretti army, so as his mate, no male would be stupid enough to look at her in that way. Not to mention, there was no infidelity in the vampire race. Once you met your mate, there was no one else. Humans wrote romance stories about this sort of thing. Vampires lived it.

Eventually.

It could just take hundreds of years until you met the one.

Some vampires had relationships of sorts. Not fake mates like Stefano had been attempting—damn psychopath—but from time to time, vampires became regular lovers. She'd heard of vamps even moving in together. It was done knowing they would each meet their mates one day and step aside when it happened. It wasn't the same as with humans. You never fell in love with someone other than your mate. Of course, you enjoyed their company, cared for them, but there would be no broken hearts in this instance.

Sofia could see the benefits. Vampires were more promiscuous than humans, so if you found someone compatible sexually, why not live together.

She'd never been free to do anything like that. Suppressed by her family, Sofia hadn't been completely inexperienced when she met Lance, but now, she couldn't keep her hands off her male.

Lance didn't seem to mind at all.

For someone like Anna, who was looking for anything to help her avoid facing her pain, these were the things Sofia would be cautious of. Sex, drugs, gambling—they were all tools for victims to use as distractions. A relationship of any kind was out of the question for Anna while she was healing. She needed time. She needed care. She needed protection.

Sofia wasn't letting any of the males near Anna until she was ready.

Anna's eyes darted around the walls and up into the

ceilings of the enormous Moretti castle. She couldn't believe she was here.

Sure, she'd lived there for months, but they'd designed the space inside the rehabilitation center so it felt like you were in any other building. Boring old white walls and ceilings. She definitely did not feel like she was in a castle.

Now she did, and it was awesome!

She felt like she'd stepped back in time. Centuries-old paintings hung on the walls, and there were statues and antique rugs wherever she looked. Even cool, embellished black *M*s on the carpet, staircases, above doorways, and other spots caught her eye.

The Morettis.

She'd met the king, and he seemed nice.

The modern things mixed with the old were so awesome. Anna spotted a digital screen on one wall sharing important messages with the staff working in the castle. Apparently, tonight's meal in the Great Hall would be chicken cacciatore.

Good to know, she smirked.

What surprised her the most was how many vampires there were everywhere. Some in uniforms like hotel housekeeping; others suited like corporate people. Then (*holy hotness!*) there were soldiers in the iconic black Moretti uniform.

Her eyes followed a group of five males walking past. The view from behind was just as delicious as the front. Those pants really knew how to show off a rear end.

Hot damn.

"Anna," Sofia interrupted her thoughts, snapping her attention back to their tour.

"Hmm? Oh, yes." Attempting to hide the grin caused by one of the males turning and winking at her, she commented, "Do you think there are any jobs available here?"

Sofia slowed down and tilted her head at her. "You want to go back to work already?"

Hells yes, if that was the type of eye candy she got to look at every day.

"Sure. I have to get on with my life, right?" She shrugged.

"No. You can take all the time you need. King Moretti has committed to provide as much resources as you all need for your recuperation."

Inwardly, she snorted.

There was no getting over what had happened to them. In any case, it had been five seconds of experience compared to the long life she would have. No point in dwelling. Anna just wished they would all stop fussing about it. She was trying her best to show them all she was fine.

Fine.

Just fucking finnneeee!

"He's so nice. I like the king," Anna said, moving the conversation along. "It would be an honor to work here, you know. And serve him. So, if you hear about any jobs, could you let me know?"

Sofia stared at her for a long moment before nodding.

"*Sì.* I will. Perhaps we can find a few things for you to do," she added.

"That would be great." Anna smiled.

She knew she wasn't a prisoner in the castle. If she wanted to, she could leave at any point. They had all been very clear with her and all the other guests about that. Some of them had already left, and Anna knew at some point she would need to move on.

Going home, though? No way.

She loved her parents, but they just didn't deal well with the messy stuff, meaning emotions. Anna understood why, but that didn't mean she wasn't angry about it. She really wanted to run into their arms and have them envelop her with all the love and safety she needed. But she knew they never would. They had nothing to give. Not since her twin sister had died, and they'd blamed themselves. Because the truth was, it *had* been their fault.

So, no, she wasn't going home.

They continued their walk around the castle for the next forty-five minutes, until her body began to ache, as it was prone to do these days. Anna wrapped her arms around her middle, and Sofia spotted it. She didn't miss a thing, and Anna was grateful because it meant she didn't have to talk about…it.

Sofia slowed. "Are you hungry?"

"Mm-hmm," she hummed, nodding. "Sure, I can eat something."

She followed Sofia into what had to be the Great Hall, as it was filled with tables of all shapes and sizes where people were dining. *Chicken cacciatore*, she smiled to herself. She could smell it.

Sofia waved out to a table of—wait, was that Princess Willow?

Holy…smokes!

"Come, Anna. Meet some of my friends."

"Your fr…?"

No. Way.

Anna had seen many of the royals at the vigil they held for those who hadn't survived…it. She was literally fangirling right now. The princess was sitting with a stunning female who had the most gorgeous red hair, and they were laughing.

"Sofia, hi!" the princess called out. She had an American accent, which surprised Anna. "Please, join us."

"Anna, this is Willow Moretti," Sofia introduced, and Anna curtsied, as was appropriate.

Willow waved her off and pointed to a seat opposite her. "Please, sit, sit. This is my bestie, Brianna."

"Hi, Anna." Brianna grinned. "Welcome to crazy town."

Anna giggled. "Hi."

Sofia ordered for them both, and the server placed drinks in front of them.

"Did you enjoy the tour?" Willow asked, continuing to eat her chicken.

Anna nodded as she drank.

"This place is incredible. It's so huge," she gushed. "I mean, obviously, it looks big from the outside, but how do you find your way around?"

Brianna grinned and leaned forward. "Don't tell my mate, but I just ask any of the pretty-looking soldiers on duty. They're always willing to help."

Willow frowned and nudged her with her arm. "You'll get them in trouble, Bri. I'm surprised they even talk to you." As Brianna shrugged, Willow glanced across the table to explain. "She's mated to Craig, the commander of the king's army."

Holy shit.

Anna's eyes widened. That male was well known to be huge and dangerous.

"The commander?"

Brianna smiled at her so brightly she nearly set the world on fire. *Wow.* One day, Anna wanted to be in love like that.

"He's—"

"Huge. Big. Scary. Yeah, yeah. I know. He's actually a teddy bear," Brianna said.

"He's really not," Willow mumbled.

Anna smiled at the two females as they continued eating their meal and bantering back and forth. They were so cool.

For a royal, Willow was very relaxed and friendly. In fact, every single Moretti she had met had been warm and kind to her. The queen she saw regularly in the rehab center, and the king had attended the vigil and visited the center once or twice. But she had never shared a meal with a royal before, so this was turning out to be the best day of her life.

She looked over at Sofia and grinned. The vampire smiled back warmly, but she could see the constant look of concern in her eyes. Anna appreciated her protection, but yeah, she just wanted to move on with her life. And some days, Sofia just reminded her of *it*.

It, which shall not be discussed.

"He's definitely not a teddy bear, but I hope he's in a good mood today," Sofia said with a slight grimace.

Brianna looked up. "Why, what's going on?"

"Ben is visiting tonight. Lance wanted to play bodyguard, but I said no. The compromise, for want of a better word, is that Craig will be making an appearance."

"God." Willow groaned.

"Yeah." Sofia nodded.

Anna looked from female to female. "Who's Ben? Your former inmate boyfriend or something?"

All of them burst into laughter. Anna grinned.

"No, Ben is my brother," Sofia explained, still laughing. "But...well, one day when you're mated, you'll understand. Trust me, it's a wonder we can pee unprotected."

"True that," Willow agreed.

"Stop. Brayden is not that bad," Brianna said.

Willow glanced quickly over her shoulder where, standing near the wall, looking relaxed but alert, two large males in black Moretti uniforms stood. She raised a brow. "Sure, okay."

Anna stared at the security for a moment.

"Are they, like, the secret service or something?"

"Yup. 'Cause I'm a princess now, so apparently, everyone wants to kill me." She rolled her eyes.

"Willow!"

"Okay, fine, so a few bad vamps did try to kill us—"

"Ah, I think we should probably change the subject," Sofia interrupted sharply. "How's the queen doing today?"

Willow paled and looked at Anna. "Oh, shit. Fuck. Sorry."

Anna looked away. It hadn't bothered her at all. Because she didn't think about *IT*.

Discussions continued around her about the queen who was heavily pregnant while Anna's mind wandered. She hated that they'd changed the subject because of her.

"It's okay," Anna suddenly burst out without thinking. They all stared at her. "It's okay. I'm okay, so you can say whatever you want."

The two females quickly looked at Sofia for guidance. It was awkward as fuck, and Anna immediately regretted it. She picked up her glass and tried to imagine she was somewhere else. Making a fool of herself in front of the princess was such an idiot thing to do.

Ugh.

Suddenly, a phone beeped.

Sofia cursed as she picked up her phone and stared at the screen.

"Damn. I didn't realize the time." She looked at Anna and chewed her lip. "My brother is here. Umm, what are we going to do…"

"I can walk Anna back to the rehab center if you want?" Brianna offered.

Anna stiffened, which Sofia noticed immediately.

Why had she reacted? She liked these females.

She looked at Sofia and gave her a small smile. She felt safe with her, and clearly wasn't as ready to step out into the big wide world as she had thought she was. Her heart sunk a little.

"No, it's fine," Sofia replied, taking charge, and Anna relaxed. "We have to go past the main entrance on the way, so I'll sign him in and then take her back."

Anna sent Brianna a small smile of apology.

"Hey, no problem." Brianna waved her off like it was no big deal.

Anna appreciated her casual brush off, but deep down, she was disappointed in herself. She hated that *it* had impacted her life.

"It was sooo nice to meet you both," Anna said, standing when Sofia did.

"Thanks, you guys," Sofia spoke, giving them a grateful smile, and then they walked out of the Great Hall.

Anna had to walk fast to keep up with the usually calm vampire; she seemed stressed. Then she remembered the conversation about her brother arriving.

"So sorry about this, Anna. It's so unprofessional of me," Sofia began. "I'll just sign Ben in, and he can wait in the foyer while I take you back. Are you okay with that?"

Anna scurried along beside her. "Of course. It's fine. Thank you for taking me around and introducing me to Willow. She's so pretty. And I love Brianna. Wow, her hair. It's beautiful."

"Yes, yes," Sofia agreed distractedly, smiling briefly.

She'd never seen the female so flustered.

As they made their way back though the corridors toward the main doors of the castle, vampires scuttled out of the way, barely giving them a second look. Well, except for one hot, uniform-clad—

"Anna!" Sofia said sharply, shaking her head. "It's best if…"

"What?"

Sofia shook her head again.

Anna frowned. It was as if the female didn't want her noticing the males. *Why?*

"Hi, hi. I'm here," Sofia called out as they reached the security team at the front door.

Anna could see a large male standing slightly behind four guards, but Sofia's head blocked Anna's view.

"Hey, Ben."

"Sign here, please, Mrs. De Luca."

Pen hit the paper, and the next minute, a lanyard was handed to the male, who walked through the doors.

Holy shit. Anna froze; all except her mouth, which dropped open.

"Hey, Sofi," Ben greeted as he pulled Sofia into a bear hug. Over her shoulder, his eyes landed on Anna's face, and it was like she had been hit with a lightning bolt.

His eyes widened slightly.

Anna felt heat creep along her cheeks and across her décolletage.

And through her veins.

My God, Ben was the most gorgeous male she'd ever laid eyes on.

Compared to the males she'd seen around the castle tonight, he was huge. Not just big; he was cut. Her friends had dated enough gym guys, so she knew the term, and this male's body was the perfect definition. His muscles weren't just huge and solid; they were defined in a way most men, and women, could only dream of.

And while his body was totally blush worthy in and of itself, it was the way his piercing eyes had looked at her which had her feeling like this.

Ben stood up and kissed Sofia on the top of her head, then his eyes darted back to Anna.

God, she wished she could stop doing the thing with her hands. Anna plunged them into her back pockets.

No, fuck, don't do that. Now she was pushing her tits out.

Ben grinned.

My fucking God, he has dimples. Shoot me now.

Her panties were instantly wet.

Anna chewed her lip and wrapped her arms around herself, giving him a small smile. She knew her cheeks were a terrible mix of red blended with peach right now. And. Wanted. To. Die.

"Ah, Ben, this is Anna," Sofia introduced, her eyes darting between them as she picked up on all the awkwardness.

"Nice to meet you, Anna," Ben said, reaching out his hand, his eyes never leaving hers.

She unwrapped her arms and wiped her sweaty palms on her jeans, and he grinned wider. She cleared her throat and smiled at him. "Hey. Hi."

Her hand reached out, and Ben's large, strong hand

enveloped hers.

A bolt of energy rushed through her, and her smile faded.

Ben took Anna's small hand in his, and his entire body lit up. A strong tingle of desire and a more powerful need overwhelmed him.

What the hell?

As her smile disappeared, they stared at each other. He was powerless to look away. How had such a small thing rendered him powerless?

Fucking hell.

Ben understood and recognized the lust. *I mean, damn, that body.* All that blonde hair and those eyes the color of the Mediterranean Sea; he could imagine her lying on white sand in a bright-red bikini, big sunglasses, and a floppy sun hat. Her reaction to him had been great for his ego, not that it needed any boosting, but it was the secondary reaction within him that was screaming at him.

And he never ignored his intuition.

It had saved his life many times before.

He felt an indescribable need to pull her into his side and fight anyone who even looked at this female. Beyond the beauty of her eyes, deep within, he saw pain. Big fucking pain.

They continued to stand there, her hand in his, him staring at her wanting answers, wanting to…goddamn it…to something. Wrap her in his arms and do all kinds of inappropriate things. No, not those. Well, yes those, but not just those.

He needed to hold her.

Take her.

Protect her.

Kidnapping his sister's friend was unlikely to get him any bonus points. Plus, he wasn't here just to see Sofia. He had a job to do. But this female had definitely thrown a spanner in the works.

He let Anna's hand go and took a small step back.

Sofia coughed.

Ben ran a hand through his hair and angled his body away from Anna. Marginally.

"So, you work with my sister, huh?" he asked, knowing she could hear a mix of American and Italian accent in his voice. He'd been living in America for over seventy years now, so while he still spoke Italian fluently, his accent had changed.

"Ah…working? Sure," Anna said, looking at Sofia as if she was uncomfortable.

What was going on, he wondered.

"Anna is in a program we're running," Sofia answered, waving her hand out all *don't worry about it*.

Ben played the game.

"Cool. How's it going?" he asked, not dropping it.

His sister should know he wasn't a male who dropped things if they caught his attention. Especially not one with a red flag waving. His instincts were sharp as a fucking knife, and something wasn't right here. As he watched Anna, he saw her eyes darting around the foyer desperately looking for a distraction.

Very fucking interesting.

Ben glanced at Sofia and narrowed his eyes slightly. She shook her head at him.

"I've been brushing up on my royal history," Anna replied finally as she looked at him again. That gorgeous blush returned.

Damn that blush. Ben wanted to run his fingers over her supple skin even though he didn't believe a single word that had just left her plump pink lips. He grinned at her instead, which only increased things over in Blushville.

"Okay, so I need to take Anna back to the…err, classroom," Sofia began. "Can you wait—ugh, God."

Ben felt the hair on the back of his neck rise in warning before he heard the voice.

"Benjamin Ferrero. Look what we have here."

Slowly, he turned to face the voice.

"Actually, it's just Ben." He grinned at the beast standing a few feet away. "But you can call me Mr. Ferrero if you want to be all formal and fuck."

"No fucks given here," Craig replied, planting his own grin in place. The guy should know it was more of a grimace; Ben doubted the guy knew how to smile.

Then the big motherfucker crossed his arms.

Bigger arms than he had, but not as defined. He smiled wider, and they both knew what his grin was about.

"What are you doing here, Ferrero?" the male asked, dropping his awkward stretched lip action.

Ben plunged his hands into his jeans pockets, which was not a smart move; it would delay him if he had to defend himself, though he was mostly sure Craig wasn't going to make a move on him, not in front of these females or civilians.

The commander had no cause to. He suspected he did, but he was wrong. They were all fucking wrong. They had no idea, and he hoped they never would if he did his job right.

"Just visiting my sister. You?"

Craig shook his head. "Don't be a fucking asshole."

"Oh, right, you work here. I forgot." He smirked, rocking on his feet like he was at a birthday party making small talk.

He heard a little noise behind him.

"Anna, it's okay. This is Brianna's mate, Craig," Sofia said, sounding anxious. "Um, guys…"

"Brianna, huh?" Ben smirked. Looking back, Ben realized it was a fucking stupid move. I mean *hello*, taunting an enormous, powerful vampire over his mate? Stupid move even for him, but the guy was pissing him off.

Anyway, hindsight was a wonderful thing. Here's what happened.

The room exploded.

Craig launched himself at Ben as he was pulling his hands out of his pockets. *Fuck*. He only just grabbed the commander before he got bowled over, and then Lance, his sister's mate, and two other big fuckers finally arrived to pull Craig off him. That wasn't a pretty sight in itself: arms and fists flying everywhere; he learned a few new curse words.

Then his world stopped.

A tiny, anguished sound, like an animal being tortured.

Ben turned.

He knew it had come from Anna.

She stood, her body shaking like a goddamn earthquake. Her face was contorted in fear, a quivery sound coming from deep within her. Ben's eyes darted to Sofia, whose mouth had dropped open. He didn't wait, he didn't think, and he didn't care. Only one thing mattered in that moment. With vampire speed, he moved across the space and pulled Anna to the floor, onto his lap, and cradled her in his arms.

He heard a sound and looked up at the bodies around

him. He had no authority in this castle or their world, but he gave zero fucks in that moment. This female needed protection, and frankly, none of them seemed to be taking her needs into consideration. He wanted to wrap her in a ball and lock her away in a tower safe from the world. And if that's what she needed, he would.

Without permission.

Because a vampire like him didn't need it. Ever.

And certainly never asked for it.

"Keep the fuck away. All. Of. You." His voice was as deadly as a male's could be.

Everyone in the room froze.

"Clear this space, now," Craig ordered, his own voice a powerful command.

"Hey, Anna. Can you look at me?" Ben asked, his voice low and gentle.

"Jesus," Craig muttered.

"Goddammit," Lance cursed simultaneously.

"Anna," Ben repeated and pushed a lock of her pretty blonde hair off her face.

"Ben, let her go. I need to get her back to the rehabilitation center," Sofia spoke as she knelt beside him.

What the fuck?

Ben cursed quietly. He bloody knew something was up.

"Rehab? Is that what they call royal history these days?" he growled quietly at his sister.

"Ben, stop!" Sofia cried. "Lance, help me get Anna."

"Nope," Lance said, shaking his head. "Let him be."

Ben continued to run his hand over her forehead and make weird cooing noises he had no idea were in his vocabulary.

Finally, Anna blinked. Her eyes began to focus on

him. He watched her take in one, two, three breaths as he rubbed her arm. "Attagirl."

"Where am I?" she asked.

"History lessons," Ben answered, smiling down at her. "Apparently."

Vincent turned the corner to see the shit show he'd just been informed about. Every single one of the survivors from the rehabilitation center was his goddamn responsibility, so when he'd heard there was an incident involving one of them, he wasn't waiting on a briefing. He teleported straight there.

"What's going on?" Vincent boomed.

And yes, thanks for asking, every-fucking-one paid attention.

Willow and Brianna came running in after him.

"Oh my God, are you okay?" Brianna cried, dropping to the floor next to Anna.

"Yes," the female said, taking a handful of the shirt belonging to the male she was sitting on and trying to pull herself up.

As any decent male would, he picked her up and placed her on her feet.

Jesus. Now that the guy was standing up, it was clear he was a big motherfucker. Vincent looked at Craig in question.

Sofia's brother, Your Majesty, Craig answered telepathically.

The male stared down at Anna and, as if no one else in the room existed, ran a hand over her arm. "Are you okay?"

She nodded, and only then did the male look up and

around. Eventually, his eyes landed on him. Because, you know, he was the fucking king.

Vincent raised a brow.

"Fucking told you," Craig said, crossing his arms.

Brayden stepped up beside him, arms on his hips. Vincent could feel the anger rolling off his brother. "Bow to your goddamn king, Ben Ferrero," the prince growled.

The male stared between him and the prince, then lowered his head.

"My apologies," Ben offered, and they all knew he meant not one fucking word. He turned to take in the female again and sent her a smile. A comforting smile. A smile with heat and heart.

Groan.

"Ben is my brother, Your Majesty," Sofia explained. "He is visiting, and—"

"We had a disagreement," Craig interjected.

"It has…upset Anna," Sofia explained. She placed a hand behind the female's back. "I'm taking her back to the center."

God, all these fucking voices.

Vincent rubbed his forehead. He could see Anna was stressing the fuck out, and Sofia was trying to help. He glanced around, taking in the situation. Fuck yeah, it would have been intimidating. Huge angry warriors surrounded her, and they were all wound up so tight someone was—*had* exploded. And that was not good enough.

These survivors, guests, needed protection, harmony, and some fucking consideration, regardless of what size boots you fucking wore.

"Okay, stop," Vincent ordered. "Craig, move your team out. Brayden, you are with me. Willow, you are supposed to be with the queen. Do. Not. Tell. Her. About.

This."

Willow nodded and took off after mouthing a *love you* to the prince.

Craig glared at him. Vincent raised a brow back, and the guy looked at Ben.

Vince sighed and stared at the male they'd all told him about. Sofia's brother. God, he hoped there were no more Ferreros for him to deal with, at least not in this century. The guy was a big-ass motherfucker, cut as fuck, and with an attitude to boot.

What did they want him to do? Put him in time-out?

What Vincent wanted to know was why Craig and Brayden hadn't recruited the guy yet. They usually did, and they took no shit. He believed they'd pound the attitude out of him in no time, but he wasn't interfering. That was Brayden's area of responsibility.

"Sofia, take Anna," he ordered, then more strongly, "Ben, please join the prince and me. You can meet with your sister once she has finished."

Sofia nodded and began to lead Anna away. The female stopped, turned, and up on her tippy-toes, placed a quick kiss on Ben's cheek. They all watched as Ben took her hips in his hands and leaned to whisper something in her ear. Anna nodded and finally left with Sofia.

Ben's eyes followed her until she disappeared. Then, his body shifted. All of the softness about him vanished. His stance changed; he stood taller, harder, and in a warrior's stance. Yet, if you didn't know what to look for, you'd think he was just hanging at the mall, all relaxed and full of bullshit.

The hair on Vincent's neck rose. He finally saw what Craig and Lance had been talking about.

This was a dangerous male. Deadly.

"Change of plans. Ask Craig to join us," he said quietly to Brayden, not taking his eyes off Ben.

"What about me?" Brianna asked.

Vincent rolled his eyes. "Go check on the reindeer."

CHAPTER NINETEEN

Halfway to Italy, 1891

"Why are we stopping?" Kate asked, looking up from her book.

Riccardo slid the heavy drapes aside, allowing him to look outside. He sat back. "The sun is going to rise very soon. We are stopping here for the day."

Kate nodded and began to pack away her book. Her sense of time was completely off, and the journey felt like it was lasting an eternity.

"Stay here. I will wake the management of the hotel, get us some rooms, and come back for you," he instructed her. Riccardo would use his mind control to ensure the driver and hotel staff weren't an issue for them, but he would do it as carefully and respectfully as possible. He would ensure they were paid and that they believed them to be good guests who had arrived earlier in the evening.

She was looking forward to having space to herself in

her own room to grieve and not cringe every time Riccardo looked over at her. Whether she would sleep or not was yet to be determined.

Every time she closed her eyes, she imagined terrible images of her parents being killed, or she saw Vincent.

Damn him.

But he was her past now. She had to focus on respecting her parents' lives. She would hold a vigil and see them put to rest in the ways of vampires.

How could this have happened?

Her parents were kind, upstanding citizens and had no enemies. Riccardo believed the attack had been done by vampires because they'd been beheaded, and were likely after their money and jewelry. But why had they left them inside the carriage, safe from the sun? There were questions that needed answering, and it was now her responsibility.

Kate's stomach turned.

She'd lost her parents and the male she thought was her mate. Just because Vincent didn't feel that way about her didn't mean she was grieving the loss any less. She didn't care if he was the king or the caretaker. She loved him. She wanted him as her mate, to be beside her in life. To support each other through these times. Now she was alone. Oh, there were family friends and other female vampires she sometimes socialized with, but no one she was very close with.

Except perhaps Riccardo. But she was beginning to feel more and more uneasy in his company.

The carriage door opened, and Riccardo held his hand out. The ground was wet, and her feet slopped into the mud. They ran across the road and into the hotel. The manager, in his sleeping clothes and holding a candle despite the place having electricity, showed them to their rooms.

"Adjoining rooms, but I daresay the door shall stay closed," he said, giving them a sharp look. "Even if you are engaged."

He scoffed and walked off.

Kate let out a half-hearted laugh when he was out of sight. Vampires found their societal rules humorous. If she'd found Riccardo attractive, she'd have had no problems warming his bed tonight. But she didn't.

He was a good-looking male, but besides the fact she was grieving her parents and nursing her shame and pain from being rejected by the king, he was not the vampire for her.

"Well, good day to you, Riccardo. Thank you." She let him unlock her door and stand aside so she could walk in. As she turned, she found him right behind her.

"Kate," he said, reaching out his hand and laying it on her upper arm.

She stiffened.

"I'm tired. My heart aches, Riccardo." She held his eyes, sending as much meaning as she could through her own, hoping he would leave.

"Let me comfort you. Hold you."

A ripple of great unease spread throughout her body.

"You have done enough. Truthfully. I would like my own company for the day, and hopefully, get some sleep."

She watched him frown, a darkness in his eyes she was becoming familiar with, then look away.

"Yes, okay. Rest, Kate. Tonight, we shall continue our journey, and when we get home, you and I shall discuss our future."

Kate pressed her lips together, nodded, and turned.

When she heard the door click, she slumped onto the bed.

Damn you, Vincent.

CHAPTER TWENTY

England, 1891

"No! Tell them we want three! One won't do. Don't they realize we are moving everything?" Vincent shouted. "And everyone!"

Regan raised his eyebrows.

Vincent spun around and fisted his hands, slamming them on the window ledge. He stared out at the driveway as if willing Kate's carriage to return.

"We can't just magic up three ships overnight, Your Majesty," Regan said.

If the male hadn't been his father's trusted advisor, Vincent would have fired him on the spot. He had little patience for anyone or anything these days. As far as he was concerned, everyone was incompetent and working against him. They were trying to muddy his plans and make life difficult.

As if it wasn't already…without *her*.

"So you're telling me there is only *one* ship in the entire English harbor? One ship? That's it?" He growled. "For God's sakes, man, pay them double. Triple. I don't care!"

Regan frowned again, turning as the prince walked through the door.

"What's the damn hurry, Vincent?"

"Three months! They want us to wait three fucking months before we depart!" he yelled, throwing his hands in the air.

Brayden glanced at Regan, and they both shrugged. "I repeat. What is the damn rush?"

He let out a long growl and planted himself in the seat behind his desk. No one would understand. He had to get out of here. Out of England.

Or he would go after her.

"Just get the fucking ships," he growled in a mutter.

CHAPTER TWENTY-ONE

Present Time

"It's Christmas Eve!" Brianna exclaimed, dancing into the room like a damn elf. Vincent shook his head as she plopped herself on Craig's lap, who had his body jammed into a beanbag which looked like it was about to explode.

Apparently, they all had to sit around this fucking tree which had sparkly shit thrown all over it and stare at it for about one hour.

This was Christmas.

The entire room, which was a large but cozy space they called the Royal Family Room, was covered in red this, green that, and silver something else. He totally didn't understand it. What the hell was a flying duck with wings and a red scarf significant of? Because it was currently hanging off a green branch and apparently *really adorable*.

Fuck me.

Vincent threw back the egg-something-or-other drink

someone had handed him. It wasn't bad, but it was missing something. "This needs some more whisky in it," he said. "Like ninety-nine percent more."

Brayden laughed and handed him the bottle.

"Was my mate always this Christmassy?" Craig asked Willow with a raised brow.

A creepy smiled spread across Willow's face as she slowly nodded.

The princess was absolutely loving the torture all three of the males were currently suffering. At times, she drove him mad, but he kept reminding himself that a weaker female wouldn't be able to handle his alpha brother. The two were perfectly matched. Vincent just had to stay one step ahead of these feminine troublemakers.

So far, he wasn't doing a great job.

He smirked to himself. They did bring some life into the castle, he hesitantly admitted to himself. Vincent had done some research. He was prepared for the Easter onslaught. With baby Moretti about to make an appearance, perhaps it would be fine. For a short while. But he wasn't letting Brianna put a flock of damn rabbits out the front of the castle.

Flock. Herd.

Whatever.

"So this is our life now," Craig muttered, burying his face into Brianna's wild hair.

"You love it," she replied, giggling.

"I love you," he growled. "Otherwise, that singing fucking reindeer would be kindling already."

Vincent snorted, but stopped abruptly. "Wait, that fucker sings as well? Get rid of it."

Kate giggled.

"I can't believe you made it to Christmas," Willow told

Kate. "Seriously, I thought the baby was going to pop out a week ago."

They all had.

Waiting was painful, and time seemed to be going really slow waiting for their child to arrive.

Kate nodded and wriggled awkwardly in the chair. "I wish it would get the hell out of me already," she said. "Nine months is a really long time, no matter how grateful you are for this blessing."

Vincent rubbed the back of her neck and she smiled up at him. He'd noticed Kate was wrigglier today than usual, and it wasn't just him keeping a side-eye on her. Every vampire in the room was.

"So what do we do now?" Vincent asked the Christmas fairies.

"Now we exchange gifts," Brianna said, crawling off her mate to begin distributing the many gifts that were wrapped under the tree. "Then we eat turkey."

"Why turkeys? What did they do wrong?" Brayden asked, taking a swig of his 99 percent eggnog.

Brianna froze.

"Er…um. I don't know why." She glanced at Willow in question, who shrugged. Brianna looked chagrined. "I'm not actually a Christmas expert."

The entire room burst into laughter, and Vincent couldn't help it. He let out a huge laugh along with them.

"Here." She thrust a box at him, and he thanked her.

As he unwrapped the box, he watched the other males do the same.

"Ah…" Brayden let out as he tossed the wrapping paper to one side and held up a large green plastic water gun. "Thanks, Santa, but you know we have real ones, right?"

Craig pulled a purple one out of his box and smirked.

"Not in here," Kate growled quickly and sent Willow a faux dark look.

"What? It was Santa, not me." Willow held up her hands and grinned.

As Brayden poured whisky into his green machine, Vincent hid his smirk. Maybe this Christmas stuff was a bit fun.

Around them, paper was tossed everywhere, and laughter filled the room.

Vincent pulled out a box the size of a shoebox and pulled the lid off.

You have got to be joking?

He lifted the solid silver ornament out of the box and held it in his hand. The entire room was silent, then he heard Kate do one of her little *awws*.

He glanced at her. "Vincent, that is stunning."

Vincent looked from Brianna to Willow. Either one of them was responsible for it, not bloody Santa as the label read, and his mate was right. It was a stunning piece of art. It was grand, regal in its own right.

But it was still a fucking reindeer. Which would probably sit proudly on his shelf in his office.

He shook his head.

They both smiled at him innocently.

"This one can stay." When they began clapping, he gave them a small smile. "Thank you. The queen is right. It is stunning."

"Okay, sexy. Open your gift," Craig indicated, pulling Brianna back onto his lap and handing her a black bag. Tissue went flying. "Aww, baby."

"Don't drop them," Craig told her, laughing as Brianna excitedly opened the lid of the little black box.

"Let me see," Willow said, leaning over. "Ohhh my

Godddd. Diamonds."

They did know that as Morettis, they were rich, right? Like fucking royals? Kabillionaires?

Even Craig had amassed a huge fortune over the years with his guidance in investing. All the senior members of his team had.

Eh, better than being spoiled brats, he figured.

Next minute, the one carat diamonds were in Brianna's ears, and Craig was looking as proud as punch for getting it right.

Vincent knew the earrings were one carat because all the males had had to have a goddamn meeting of the minds to make sure they got the right gifts for their females. God forbid they get it wrong. It had been like a fucking strategy meeting with charts and shit.

"Open yours," Brayden told Willow.

Paper went flying, and this time, it was a little teal box. All the females in the room gasped loudly.

Good grief. The website had been right.

"Oh my God," Willow cried.

"You haven't even opened it yet," Brayden said, crunching his eyes in confusion. Willow and Brianna stared at him like he'd grown horns. "Sorry, Christ. Just open it already."

The room was quiet as the little box squeaked open.

Willow's mouth dropped open.

"What is this?"

"You know what it is, Willow," Brayden said, all humor leaving his face as he pulled her onto his knee. He took the five carat—again, he knew because this had been a *major* discussion—diamond ring from the box and slid it on to Willow's finger.

"But…" Willow began, tears building in her eyes.

"I know you wanted a ring, sweetheart. You are a terrible liar." He grinned at her, but there was love pouring from his brother's eyes. Willow threw her arms around him, and they could all hear her little *thank you* and *love yous*.

Brayden had shared that his mate had said she didn't need an engagement or wedding ring now that she was a vampire, but Brayden had followed her Instagram account and she had *hearted* (whatever that meant) no less than one hundred different rings in the past few months. Plus, he'd found a handful of jewelry brochures in her wardrobe.

"Do you want a ring?" Craig asked Bri suddenly.

She shook her head.

"Nope. I had the wedding experience with my husband. It's different for Willow; she never got to do it when she was human." Brianna's husband had died in Afghanistan a year before she met Craig.

"That's true. I tried to pretend I didn't care, but I love it, Bray," she said, all emotional, twirling her hand in the air.

"You know I'd give you the fucking moon if I could," Brayden growled into her hair.

Craig gagged and Brianna giggled, slapping his chest.

"I suppose you got me a toaster," Kate said, poking her tongue at him.

"What? Why would I do that? We have ten chefs in the kitchens," he replied, hand on his chest, all mock offended. "And I'm far more romantic than that."

He lifted her gift and held it up in the air, just out of reach.

The queen laughed.

"Yes, you can be when you want to. Now hand it over," she ordered him. Vincent leaned in and kissed her lips. He placed the large square box in her lap.

"Oooh, it's heavy," she said and began ripping the paper off.

The females leaned in closer.

Vincent's heart slammed against his chest. Fuck, he hoped she liked it. He wasn't good at this stuff. He hadn't shared his gift ideas with the other males and had ignored their advice. He and Kate had been mates for over one hundred and thirty years. He'd gifted her jewelry, perfume, paintings, antique vases, and every damn thing he could think of over the years. And he knew her. She wanted nothing but his love. And to have his child, which was on its way posthaste.

Kate pulled the wrapped item out of the cardboard box, glanced up at him, and then began to pull the tissue paper off it.

"Oh my!" she cried. Tears sprang to her eyes. "Vincent, it's beautiful!"

Fucking, YES! He grinned at the other males proudly, and they laughed.

"Is that a bear?" Willow asked, confused.

Kate continued turning the large glass teddy bear around in her hands, her mouth parted. It was about the size of a loaf of bread, with subtle colors on the tips of its ears, eyes, whiskers, and paws, but otherwise, it was just clear blown glass.

The famous artist had signed the bottom of it.

"It's handblown Murano glass. A bear," Vincent stated. "I had it custom made."

"It's exquisite, Vince," Kate replied, her voice in awe.

"I don't get it," Craig said, leaning forward.

Kate looked up as if realizing where she was. She laughed.

"Oh. None of you have seen our baby room." Kate

shook her head laughing. "It's decorated in bears. Teddy bears. This father-to-be"—she nudged him—"has been taunting me about the bears for months. But I love them. Plus, they're gender neutral."

Vincent leaned back in his chair. Damn gender. He really wanted to know if he was having a little boy or girl. The suspense was killing him.

Kate stood and placed the more-than-she'll-ever-know-how-expensive bear on the mantelpiece and handed him a gift.

"I have everything I want," he said, running his hand over her luscious bottom.

"No, I don't think you do." She grinned. "You just don't know you need this yet."

He ripped open the packaging and pulled out two black items. One was a T-shirt with *I make cute babies* written on it.

"Yet to be determined." Craig smirked.

"Snap," Brayden said, and they high-fived each other.

Vincent glared at them.

"Soo cute," Brianna wooed, and he rolled his eyes.

As Kate laughed, he pulled out the second item. He spotted the embroidered Moretti *M* on it and glanced at his mate, his brows pulled together. "Is this a scarf?"

She shook her head, took it from him, and began wrapping it around his body. He looked up as the girls began to snigger.

"It's a Moretti baby wrap."

Brayden threw his head back laughing.

"What? What for? I'm not taking the damn baby to work, Kate," Vincent spluttered, looking at her in horror.

She smiled and sat back in her chair.

"I'm not wearing a baby scarf," he stated, pulling it

off. "If I am holding our child, I think my arms are quite strong enough, thank you."

Kate winked at him. "Keep a hold of it, *Daddy*."

"Don't daddy me or I'll drag you up to our bedroom," he grumbled as Brayden spurted his drink out. "I need more of that egg shit. Hand me the whisky. And are we done here?"

"Christmas turkey time!" Brianna said, jumping up.

Fuck's sakes.

He'd forgotten about the meal.

Two and a half long hours later, they finally got back to their wing of the castle.

"I'm going to have a shower," Kate said, walking slowly up their stairs.

"Okay, babe, I'll be up in a minute." Vincent dropped their gifts on the table and picked up the white mug he'd also unwrapped, letting out a laugh.

King Dad it said on it, Brayden's poor humor.

While he still found Christmas to be a strange human holiday, he was beginning to understand why they liked it. It had brought joy into their already happy home. He loved giving gifts, especially to his mate; not that he needed a date to do that. That part was definitely more fun than staring at the plastic *singing* reindeer.

He walked into the steamy bathroom and ripped off his clothes.

"Hey," Kate said as he stepped under the water and wrapped his arms around her. "I'm surprised you can still do that."

He kissed the back of her neck. "You're not that big."

"Compared to you," she said, arching into his touch.

"That's right." His hand slid over her belly and down between her legs. "Spread for me, sweetheart."

Kate moved her leg to the side, but he could feel her imbalance. Not wanting to hold her too hard at this point in her pregnancy, he moved her to the wall. Their shower was spacious with seven—no, eight different showerheads pointed at different angles. He'd had a deep seat installed so he could place his queen on it and enjoy her, and you bet they used it regularly.

He lifted her onto it.

"Oh God, Vince," she cried, ready for him so quickly at this point in her pregnancy.

"Wider, baby," he requested as his thumb caressed her clit. Then he knelt as the water rushed over his ass and began to lap at her swollen flesh. Kate gripped a handful of his hair as he pressed two fingers inside her and felt his cock twitch and swell, wanting to be where his mouth was.

He sucked and licked with vigor, coaxing the pleasure from his queen as his finger worked her.

"Yes, yes, yes."

"Don't come yet," he ordered, knowing he had full command of her orgasms. "Let me taste you some more, and then I am going to fuck you."

The tightness on his hair increased. "Please, I need…"

"Do as I tell you, Kate," he commanded, reaching to stroke his cock. "Good girl."

Lick, lick.

He loved having total control, and she loved him having it.

"Squeeze your nipples for me."

She leaned back and took her breasts in her hands, tweaking them.

"Harder," he said as he strummed her clit with his tongue. "That's it, good girl."

Kate arched as her body began to tremble with the need for release, and his cock jerked in response. "Do you want the magic wand or my cock?"

"I don't care, just fuck me," Kate cried.

He took her chin. "Answer me. Tell me what you want."

Panting, Kate glanced around. She wanted to play. He reached up onto their toy shelf and pulled down the black dildo.

"Cock, I need your cock."

"Too late," he said, turning it on and rubbing the head of it over her folds. Around and around he went in circles.

Kate thrust her tits into his face as she arched more. He held the side of her belly, moving the dildo around expertly. He leaned in and sucked hard on one nipple, catching her eye as she screamed.

Then he pressed it inside her, and she cried out louder.

God, he loved fucking her with their range of sex toys. Watching the devices slide in and out of her, whether she was doing it or he was, was powerfully arousing. In her early days of pregnancy, they'd played with butt plugs, which had only tightened her more around his cock.

"I'm going to come on your pussy while I fuck you with the toy," he ground out, reaching down to jerk himself off.

Stroke, stroke.

Fuck, he really was going to come fast.

"God, Vincent, fuck me," Kate cried.

He squirted over her pussy while skillfully pressing the black dildo in and out of her.

Picking her up, he carried Kate out to their bed.

Shoving pillows into a pile, he laid her over them.

"Your cock, now," Kate begged. "Now, Vincent."

"Ass up," he ordered as he nudged her legs apart. "Fuck."

He ran his fingers through her pussy, then with his hand on his cock, directed his swollen head inside.

"Yes!" she cried.

"Tell me if I hurt you."

"Get deep inside me or I will fucking kill you," she growled, and he laughed.

He pressed his hot flesh deep and long inside her. Inch by inch, she took more of him. Pulling out, he did it again.

"My. God," Kate cried.

"Okay?"

"More. Now." She clenched around him, and damn, she'd been doing her exercises.

"Do that again," he ordered.

Kate clenched again.

"Fuck, yes," he growled as he lifted her body against him and sucked her neck. "Keep doing that."

Remaining deep inside her, he kept thrusting in small movements as she continued to clench and milk his cock while he trembled at the erotic sensation.

"*Motherfucker.*"

"God," Kate cried.

"More," he demanded. "More, Kate." Pleasure roared through his body as he gripped a boob and reached down to rub her clit.

"Holy fuck." Vincent thrust in when Kate's orgasm ripped through her, her sex gripping his cock and setting off his own hot release. Collapsing on the pillows beside her, Vincent lay facing Kate, both of them naked and dopey for a long while after. He kissed her about twenty-five times on the nose and lips. Each time, she just smiled at him.

God, he loved this female.

"Ready to be a daddy?" she asked quietly.

He nodded.

"You're going to be a wonderful father."

Vincent had gone through all the emotions over the last several months. Fear, panic, acceptance, excitement, and back to fear again. Each time, he landed on two trains of thought: One, that Kate would be an amazing mother, so even if he was useless as fuck, it didn't matter. The second was that he'd been blessed with an amazing father, so if he followed in his footsteps, he was confident he wouldn't mess it up too much.

"Either way, I have no doubt you will be the best mother," he told her, running his hand over her face. "You already are."

"Don't throw the baby wrap away, King Moretti." She grinned, "Trust me on this one."

He mock rolled his eyes, and she laughed, snuggling into him.

"The baby is coming today," she casually said.

He smiled.

Wait. What?

He jumped up and stared down at her. "What?"

She smiled up at him. "It's fine. We have time."

"No, we don't. What? When? How…" He started pacing on the spot, running his hand through his hair. "Brayden!"

Kate sat up and laughed.

"You might not want the prince for this. I know you two are close, but do you really want him looking at my cooch?"

His mouth fell open.

"Lie back down. We have time," Kate said, patting the bed.

And he did not lay back down.

CHAPTER TWENTY-TWO

England, 1891

Brayden walked up to the door and took a long breath. He really didn't want to do this, but sometimes, you just had to intervene. They'd all seen it before, many times, but as far as mated or mating males went, Vincent had to be the dumbest fucking idiot out there.

In the beginning it had been funny. At least he and Craig had enjoyed some hilarious moments watching from the sidelines. Then he'd seen Kate suffer, and now his brother, and all humor had disappeared.

Brayden knew his brother. Vincent was not an asshole; in fact, he was quite the opposite. He had more compassion for females than most of the males in the castle. Probably because in his eyes, every vampire was his.

But where Kate was concerned, he was a first-class idiot.

He'd been sure the king would come flying out of the

castle the day her carriage had departed. He'd even had a bet with Craig, which he fucking lost, that Vincent would follow her within two days. When he hadn't, they'd all sat down over a few ales and scratched their heads.

"Maybe we were wrong," Craig pondered.

"As the most recent mated male among us," Tom spoke up. "I'd agree he is mating. But fuck me, he's in major denial."

They all nodded.

"Honestly, yours was bad enough. God, it looks painful. I hope it never happens to me," Brayden said, shaking his head. He'd watched many of his friends and colleagues mate over the years, and rarely was it smooth sailing.

Tom had been fortunate with Lucinda. It had happened very quickly, which was fortunate because she was a Russo: Roberto Russo's daughter, their archenemy; though he was now dead at Brayden's fathers' hand after he had challenged him for the throne. Now Lucinda's three brothers were continuing the rebellion, with her older brother Stefano in what appeared to be a leadership role.

They had their eyes on him.

Lucinda had left the family fold and now resided in the castle with Tom, working for the king.

God, if their mating had dragged on as long as Kate and Vincent's was, it would have been a bitter battle for them all. Not that it had been all rainbows and teddy bears. At all.

Tom laughed. "I'll remind you of that one day. But yeah, it's not easy," Tom admitted, sobering fast and rubbing his hand over his jaw. "Fucking not easy at all."

No, thanks.

Brayden was happy getting his cock serviced by all the

gorgeous males and females who waved their farewells, flushed with the remnants of their orgasms, as they promptly left afterward.

Plus, he had his orgies, and they were a beautiful thing.

Brayden particularly liked the new feature he'd had installed recently. A solid member hidden away in a roll-out drawer, which one could pull out and impale a female on.

God, he loved it.

Only recently, he'd selected a female for a private session. With the water feature flowing and the candles flickering, her golden skin had glowed deliciously as he warmed her up.

Licking her from top to bottom, he'd fingered her pussy until she was wet and gasping.

"Do you want to play, little one?"

"Yes, prince. Let me service you," she'd begged.

"Not me, precious, I want to watch you fuck one of my toys," he said, gripping her chin. "Will you do that for me?"

Of course she nodded. They all wanted to please him. He didn't want to lie; that got him seriously aroused.

He took her hand and led her over to the side of the room, pulling out the drawer. The solid white molded cock sat tall and proud.

Brayden heard her little gasp and took one of her breasts in his hand. "My lord, that's…big."

"I know you can take it. You are wet and ready for it," he assured, sliding his finger into her pussy once more. "I'm going to stand here and watch you."

He nudged Elizabeth, or maybe it was Marie, on the bottom, and she licked her lips with a little glint in her eye.

Brayden smiled, rubbing his cock.

Yes. He knew he'd selected the right female for this bit

of fun.

She stepped over and grabbed it, studying its girth. Then she turned to face him, backing over it.

"That's it. Line your pussy up."

Elizabeth-Marie slid her fingers inside herself and spread her juices, preparing her body. His cock jerked, so Brayden took it in his hand and began rubbing it up and down.

Fuck me.

"Good girl. Now sit down on the cock for me. Slowly, take it inch by inch."

She did as she was told. Her knees bent as the white, bulging head entered her pussy, moaning as she took more of it inside her until, finally, she let out a long groan.

Fucking hell, this was a wet damn dream.

Brayden spied her rock-hard nipples and wanted them in his mouth. Harder and harder, he stroked his cock, come leaking from its head. His eyes darted to her pussy and back to her mouth, then down again.

"Pinch your nipples," he ordered.

He could have tied her arms in the straps he'd had installed, but he was playing. That would be another night. Or if she disobeyed.

"Now ride it. I want you to fuck it."

Using her legs, she rode the solid member, taking her breasts in her hands, gasping as she began to fuck the cock faster. She lost eye contact with him as her eyes rolled back. "Yes, oh God, my prince, *fuck*," she cried.

Her body trembled as her orgasm screamed out of her.

Fuck me.

"My, my, what do we have here?" He heard from behind him, and Brayden grinned.

Craig stepped up beside him, his own heavy cock in

hand.

"A shiny new toy."

Craig grinned. "May I?"

Jesus, Brayden was close to spurting. This was going to take it to a whole other level.

"Taste her."

Craig stepped forward and knelt, licking the female's pussy as her orgasm leaked out of her.

"De-fucking-licious."

Brayden stepped forward and grabbed a nipple, twisting it. He could see Elizabeth-Marie was in her own pleasure zone, being fucked by the two powerful vampires. "Fuck me with your mouth," he ordered, pressing his red, swollen cock into her mouth. In and out he thrust, holding her head as he went deep down her throat.

He looked down, watching Craig suck on her clit, his hand around the rear filling her. He was a goner. His seed poured into her mouth.

When he pulled out, he could see the wild need in the commander's eyes.

"Shall we take this to the sofa?"

"Fuck yes," Craig agreed, lifting the female respectfully off the white cock. "You ready for some big cock now, Marie?"

Okay, Marie it was then…

Not enough.

Brayden followed the two of them to the large sofa and watched as Craig flipped her onto her knees.

"Take me in your mouth, sweetheart," Craig said, perching on the back and spreading his legs. "And the prince can get his cock in from behind.

Christ. He loved sharing with this guy. He knew how to fuck right.

Hard again, Brayden ran his hand up and down his cock and placed himself behind her. Pressing two fingers into her ass, Marie tried to fling her head back, but Craig gripped her hair in his hand. He winked at Bray just as he thrust his thick, heavy cock into her tight cunt.

"Touch your clit," Craig instructed her, guiding her head up and over his cock.

Brayden watched, plunging in and out of her, as his friend fucked her mouth, fucking both her holes.

"Fuck me," he cried as his cock spilled once more.

"On my cock, now," Craig ordered, flipping the female like a pancake and flopping on the sofa cushions. He glanced at Brayden, and they both knew the fun had just begun.

And damn, he'd been right. Brayden intended to keep choosing delicious moments like those for as long as he could. But for now, he had to intervene and get Kate and Vincent together. A king without his queen was a…grumpy motherfucker.

"Brayden, just fucking knock and get in here."

I rest my case.

He opened the door and found his brother sitting in an armchair with a whisky.

"So you don't knock anymore?"

"You knew I was there." He laughed and planted himself in a chair. "And since when did we drink at"—he looked at his watch—"one in the morning?"

Vincent tossed it back. "Since I became king and did whatever I fucking wanted."

He narrowed his eyes. "Have you actually slept since…"

"Since? What's with all the *sinces*?"

"What?" Brayden asked, his forehead puckered.

"What."

"Have you slept?"

Vincent shrugged before walking across the room and pouring another three fingers.

"*Since* Kate left?"

The king turned and glared at him, pointing. "Do not say her name."

Brayden shook his head and stretched out his legs. He wasn't leaving until this was resolved *or* the king *actually* threatened to remove his head, a possibility for the first time in their whole lives. The guy was unstable and mating, but who else could do this? It was either him or no one. And they couldn't have an unstable king threatening people over ships and shit.

"I will say her name, and you need to face what's going on, Vince."

Another pour.

"Vincent!" he said louder.

"Go away."

Brayden ran his hand over his face. Time for dirty tactics. If Vincent was trying to bury his head in the sand and pretend Kate no longer existed, Brayden was here to fuck up his plan. Because it wouldn't work. A male couldn't exist without his mate and remain sane for long.

And clearly, the king's sanity was fading fast.

"Well, she's probably fucking Riccardo right now, in any case," Brayden casually said.

The whisky shot down the king's throat, and he poured another one.

And now, for his killer move…

"A pussy like that has to taste like goddamn strawberries. What—"

And cue the angry flying king.

The crystal glass in his hand shattered, and the next minute, Brayden was up against the wall. And goddamn it, he was working really hard to keep the smile off his face. It was only the fact this *was* bloody serious that made him be able to do so.

Vincent's eyes bulged from their sockets, his breath rich with whisky.

"Do NOT speak of her."

"Her wet pussy?" Brayden croaked, smirking.

He didn't particularly want to die, but he had a job to do. His father had told them to look out for one another, and right now, Vincent was a blind man.

"Wet, juicy pussy needing a big, long fuck," Brayden taunted, really wishing he didn't have to think about Kate's lower bits.

Further up the wall he went. "Stop it, Brayden. Fuck you!"

Okay, enough playing. He'd had enough. Brayden whacked Vincent's arms, and he dropped to the ground. He pushed the king a few steps away and straightened his shit.

"You know, while we wait for the ships, I think I'll organize a short trip to Rome. See if Kate's been serviced." This time, he jumped to the left as Vincent tried to grab him. "One look at my cock, and she'll be all over it."

Leap.

"Perhaps I'll take a few of the males." He tilted his head. "You think she's into threesomes?"

"Fuck you!" Vincent yelled, jumping over the sofa and chasing him up the stairs.

"Or likes it in the rear?" Brayden called as he leaped back down onto the ground floor.

Things were cracking and breaking around them, but needs must and all that.

"If you touch her, I'll fucking kill you!" Vincent swore, dropping beside him in a crouch.

Now Brayden was done playing. He grabbed the king and slammed him against the wall. His fangs came out as he stared into the surprised face of his brother.

He knew about the blood. Of course he did; he was a Moretti. But Brayden was stronger. They both knew it, but rarely did they test it, and never had he exhibited this power in front of anyone else. Craig thought he knew, but he didn't; though if anyone strongly suspected, it was the commander.

It didn't matter; he trusted the male with his life.

But no one knew, and no one would ever fucking know.

"Get the fuck off me, Brayden," Vincent growled. "Now."

"No. Right now, I am your brother," he growled back. "And you are *not* the king."

"I am always the fucking king. Step the fuck back."

Brayden wasn't interested in this conversation. Vincent was trying to distract him and redirect the conversation, but they were going to talk about Kate whether he liked it or not.

"Stop talking. Now, get your head out of your ass. Go to Rome and go get your mate," Brayden growled. "Otherwise, you are no use to any of us as king."

"Fuck you."

Brayden dropped him on the ground and walked back into the living area, taking in the damage they'd created. He picked up a chair and righted it.

"I'm serious," Brayden said, kicking the coffee table

pack in place.

"She's not my mate. I'd know," Vincent growled.

Brayden let out a sigh.

"Bullshit. Everyone in the castle knows Kate's your fucking mate. Every-fucking-body."

Vincent kicked the sofa, and it bolted across the floor. "I asked her to come to America, and she declined!" he shouted.

Brayden crossed his arms and stared at him.

"Look, I don't know how this love shit works, but did you...you know?"

"What?" Vincent asked, eyebrow raised.

"I don't know..." Brayden shrugged then frowned. "Maybe we need Tom here."

"The fuck? No. I don't need Tom," Vincent shouted. "I...I just asked her."

Brayden pursed his lips. "With flowers and stuff?"

Vincent frowned.

"No. I asked her to come...as you know, a friend."

"Oh. My. Fucking. God!" Brayden cried, throwing his arms in the air. "Jesus, save me! Do you or do you not want to fuck that female?"

Dark eyes darted at him.

"That!" He pointed at his brother. "That's the crazy mating look."

"I am not going to have sex with Kate only to break her heart when my mate comes along," Vincent said, exasperated.

Brayden ran a hand through his hair and let out a frustrated growl.

"Alright. Let me get my crayons and paint you a goddamn picture," he told his glaring brother. "Another male bending Kate over and fucking her."

"I warned you," Vincent growled.

God, give me strength. Please don't let me be this completely fucking stupid when I eventually meet my mate.

"You love her," Brayden spelled out, going for all the feels now. "If no other male can touch her, it means you love her."

Vincent shook his head. "I've checked the mirror; my eyes have not changed."

Brayden flung his head back. A mated male and female's eyes ended up with a dark ring around them once mated; it was always one of the last signs. It was not a reason to walk away from the vampire you could barely breathe without.

It was official. His brother was a moron.

"Right now, Riccardo is making a move for Kate," Brayden said as Vincent's eyes darted to his. "He told Craig and me he was going to make her his. He's going to move her into his family home and, well, fuck her brains out, I guess."

Brayden watched as Vincent's face turned from red to some kind of purple color.

Fina-fucking-lly!

"Get your team, and where the fuck is Regan?" Vincent yelled as he marched out the door. Then he stopped, turned, and pointed a finger at him. "If you are lying or fucking wrong about this so help me God…"

Brayden grinned.

"Regan!" the king roared.

Two hours later, they were on their way to Rome.

Craig was leading, then Vincent, Brayden, Tom, and

two of their senior lieutenants at the rear, all on a mission to get their queen. Or at least, that's what Brayden hoped.

"You have her address?" Vincent called out for the third time.

"Yes, Your Majesty." Tom winked at Brayden, and they shared a grin.

"We'll have to stop—" someone started.

"We are not stopping!" Vincent ordered, digging his heels into the side of his horse, sending him into a gallop.

The rest of them followed suit and rode without rest to get the girl.

Literally.

CHAPTER TWENTY-THREE

Rome, 1891

Kate pulled the heavy curtains in the living room and stared out at the garden. Beyond the gates of her family home, the streets of Rome were quiet. Unsurprising, given it was early morning.

They had arrived home over an hour ago, and she'd finally encouraged Riccardo to leave. His subtle touches and sudden protectiveness would have been fine if they'd felt brotherly, but they both knew they weren't.

She didn't have the strength right now to say anything, but if he crossed the line, she would.

It had come close when he'd come into her hotel room before nightfall to see if she was ready to leave. Kate had slept in late and was still in her thin white nightgown. She'd seen his eyes staring at her breasts as her nipples pressed against the cotton in the cool evening air.

"*I see you need more time*," he'd said.

She'd nodded. "*I fell asleep late. I'm sorry.*"

"*No apology needed,*" Riccardo had assured, taking a step toward her. "*Kate, if—*"

"*We should hurry. We have a long night ahead of us. I shan't be long,*" she had interrupted, turning to gather her clothing. A glance over her shoulder had shown her the tension on his jaw just before he turned to leave.

Now she was on borrowed time.

With no brother, no father, and no one to provide for her, Kate would have to take a look at her family's finances and make some decisions for her future. They were not a poor family, she knew that, but a female living alone in the middle of Rome was not acceptable. They did, after all, live in a human world.

Riccardo would insist on her moving in with him eventually, she knew he would, and that would include having sex with him.

A tear slid down her face.

He wasn't a horrible-looking male; she could do worse. Perhaps she would even enjoy it from time to time.

She had to make some decisions. If her mate didn't want her—if Vincent had even been her mate—then there would be no other.

The next evening, Kate finally saw the last of her visitors out, a mix of human and vampires, all bringing food and flowers. They had come to show their respects after the tragic loss of her parents.

Her home looked like the florist shop, and all she wanted to do was toss them in the fire.

Riccardo had stayed by her side all evening. It had

been both a comfort and irritation. She appreciated the friendship, but acting like her mate or husband was not what she had invited him to do. Kate had just smiled at the *he's a lovely man, isn't he* whispers and knowing smiles from the women.

All she wanted was some privacy to grieve her parents. Her heart was breaking with grief, and yet, life with all its expectations didn't disappear or wait for her.

But no one understood her secret. Her heart had been broken twice. For a vampire, to lose their mate was devastating.

"Kate, I think you should ease up on the sherry," Riccardo said.

She didn't even like the goddamn sherry. It had been her mother's, so she'd poured herself one. It was sweet and easy to drink, so she'd kept on it all evening, enjoying the richness.

Anyway, it took a lot for a vampire to get drunk.

"I think—oh," she began, stopping when Riccardo held up the crystal decanter with only an inch left in the bottom.

Kate sat on the sofa and sighed.

"A long evening," Riccardo said, leaning against the fireplace.

"Yes."

She'd been through her family documents later in the day, after waking, and while things weren't bad, they weren't good either. Her father owned mostly assets which he'd built up over the past five hundred years. He had earned income, which paid for the running of the household, working as an accountant for Count Mozzi.

With no income and no skills with which to find a job, Kate was pushed into a corner. There was some cash in the coffers, but not enough to last her more than a few months.

She would have to sell the house and move out into the country where she could live a quieter life. The money would last her a long while, but not forever. When you were immortal, you had to think much further ahead.

Perhaps she would go to America after all.

"I can see your mind racing, Kate."

She nodded.

He moved across the room and sat next to her, taking her hand. "I promise to look after you."

She turned her face to look at him. Could she? Could she be with him?

Tears formed in her eyes.

Riccardo cupped her face. "Hey. *Mamma* wants you to move in, and so do I." He smiled. "Why don't we pack your things up tomorrow."

What other choice did she have? It was now or later. Kate didn't have the energy to fight him, so she nodded.

"Good girl." He leaned in and pressed his lips against hers gently.

A cry caught in her throat.

He applied a little more pressure and put a hand on her thigh. "Open for me, Kate."

Her eyes wide, she stared at Riccardo in surprise at his assertiveness. She'd never seen him act so bold. He smiled. "Just your lips, darling. Just your lips for tonight."

She turned away from him. He gently cupped her face and turned her back. "Let me have your mouth."

Kate opened to speak, and he misread her actions. His tongue plowed inside as he held her head. She froze and tried to push him away, but while Riccardo wasn't a large male like the Morettis, he was still stronger than her.

When he'd had enough, he released her and smiled. "Kitten, my God, you are going to be wild." He looked thrilled. "I can't believe I waited so long."

"No—"

"I need to return to the house, but I will come for you tomorrow. And Kate," Riccardo paused, running his hand over her leg. "I promise to spend hours pleasing you. I am hard for you right now, but I know you are grieving."

She swallowed.

How did she get here? It just wasn't right. She couldn't do it. Kate didn't want his hands on her at all. Not a finger.

She needed to fix this. She needed to tell him she wasn't attracted to him or wanted him in that manner. Kate went to speak again, flushed with frustration.

Riccardo took her face and plunged in again. "Gods, I want you. Look at you, pink with need. I don't think either of us can wait. My cock can't," he said, beginning to bunch up her skirts.

"What are you—"

He got on his knees. "Let me lick your cunt. I can give you this, Kate. Some pleasure right now."

She pushed her skirts down and Riccardo grinned, taking her resistance for shyness. With strength, he spread her legs apart and ran his hand up the inside of her bloomers.

"Riccardo, no."

"Don't be bashful, Kate. God, I can feel your heat." He groaned, his hand getting way too close for comfort.

Kate tried to scuttle backward, but he held her in place. A cold shiver ran through her body. She gripped the sofa, struggling to get away from him.

Then she felt it; his fingers at her core.

"Fuck me," he cried. "I need my mouth on you…my

tongue inside your pussy."

Bang bang.

"Kate. Kate!" a voice she recognized called out.

What on Earth? Was that…?

"*Just knock, for God's sake,*" another voice said, and her eyes widened.

"*No, would you…fuck, let me…*"

Vincent?

Riccardo sat back on his heels, eyes wide. He stood.

Kate pulled her skirts down and moved to get past Riccardo.

"Stop," he ordered, grabbing her arm. "What is the king doing here?"

"Vincent!" she yelled, holding Riccardo's stare.

What was the king doing here?

The question was a good one, and her mind raced from dread to hope. But right now, as a matter of urgency, she needed to get away from Riccardo. His actions had been unacceptable. She could still feel his touch between her legs and felt revolted. She hated that she was wet, but she had been dying for relief since her moment with the king.

Kate knew she should have been stronger, but she had needed his friendship. Though not enough to let him force himself on her.

The look in his eyes scared her.

She shook off his arm at the same time the front door burst open. Vincent came storming into the room, followed by the prince, Craig, and Tom. Behind them were two others she didn't recognize.

"Kate," the king said, his eye blazing.

"Your Majesty," she replied, blushing and holding his eyes for a moment, hoping to portray her need for him.

Then she curtsied.

Vincent took in the scene around him. The house was of a high standard. Large for Rome, but he knew her family was wealthy. The room was filled with flowers which he gathered were from those grieving the loss of her parents. Empty plates and glasses sat around, showing she had been entertaining.

And Riccardo.

Standing near Kate as if she belonged to him.

Vincent growled.

Had the male stood by her side as her mate this evening? The blood in his body boiled at the thought. But there was more to this. Something didn't feel right. He'd heard her angst from outside and could all but smell Kate's fear.

The male was standing far too close to her for a normal conversation, and there was a look in Riccardo's eyes—a mix of lust, confusion, and anger—which was infuriating him. Vincent wanted to slap the guy around the chops.

"What the hell is going on?" he demanded.

He took a long draw of breath and smelled lust.

"My king," Riccardo greeted, doing a really fucking fancy bow.

"I asked a question," he said loudly, stepping forward and leading Kate toward a chair. Feeling her shiver under his hands made him even more furious. As she sat, he knelt down and stared into her eyes. "Are you okay?"

Her eyes darted over to Riccardo's and back to him.

"Look at me, not him. Are you okay?"

Kate nodded.

The lust wasn't coming from her, but it lingered.

"Do you want him to stay?"

She shook her head.

That was all he needed to know. As king of the race, he couldn't plummet the guy to his death, as tempting as the idea was, so instead, Vincent stood and turned to the prince. Behind him stood Craig. He caught his eye. "Get that door fixed and tell the males to tend to the horses."

"Yes, sire." Craig disappeared.

"We will be staying here for a few days. Assuming you can accommodate us?" he asked Kate.

"Yes. Of course, Your Majesty." She nodded.

Riccardo cleared his throat.

Vincent raised a brow and turned.

"Right, yes. Well, Your Majesty, Kate is moving into my home tomorrow. We were just discussing the details."

Vincent narrowed his eyes and looked down at Kate.

"*Oh, fuck*," Brayden muttered behind him.

"Is this true?" he asked, really loudly. Had he mistaken her interest in removing the male from her home?

Kate's hands clenched the arms of her chair and stared at the faces around her. Her eyes went from face to face, looking for answers.

What the actual fuck?

She was not fucking moving in with this male. How could she even consider it? Fury boiled inside him. His fists bunched at his sides, and he was seconds from doing something he knew he'd regret. He took a few breaths and then turned.

"Go home," he ordered Riccardo.

When he didn't move, Brayden stepped forward. "Do as the king tells you."

The male nodded and looked at Kate. She didn't look

at him, but if she had, she would have seen a glimpse of threat, of control, which he hoped would have scared her.

God knew what had happened in this room tonight, but whatever it was, it was now over.

"Go," Vincent said again, his voice dark and low. "All of you, get the fuck out of this room. NOW!"

Kate swallowed and watched him. Their eyes locked together.

"Let's go," Brayden ordered, ushering them all out. Just as he heard the door being pulled closed, Brayden added, "Don't fuck this up. Either of you. Please."

Kate's head swiveled between them, her brows furrowed.

And then it was just the two of them.

Kate fell back into the chair when the door closed and stared at the king. He looked furious but relieved. He knelt down in front of her again and stared.

Suddenly, tears pooled in her eyes and began to pour down her face.

He looked horrified.

"Kate," he whispered softly, reaching for her, and she threw herself into his arms.

It was a momentary lapse of judgment she would kick herself for later, but right now, she just needed to feel safe. And it was in this male's arms she felt safest.

Vincent lifted her into his arms and sat back down in the chair as she pressed her face into his shoulder and cried.

God, she felt like a child.

"Do I need to behead him?" Vincent asked. "Because

I fucking will."

She let out a sniffly laugh and shook her head. Although it was tempting to say yes after Riccardo's behavior, she knew she was partly responsible for not drawing a line when he'd begun to cross it.

"No," she replied, lifting her head. "But I cannot stay here any longer, Vincent. I think"—she let out a little cry—"I think I may have to take you up on your offer to go to America."

He tilted his head and smirked.

Did he think this was funny?

"You make it sound like a prison sentence, Kate," he teased, letting out a little laugh. "Am I that horrible?"

She shook her head. "No, of course not. I just…well, I don't really have a choice."

She wasn't going to say he was the most handsome and sexy man she'd ever seen in her life.

"Wait, why are you here?" she suddenly asked.

Vincent frowned at her, ignoring her question. "Tell me why you have no choice. This home is yours now, is it not?"

Ahh, royalty. Completely disconnected with reality. Kate shook her head.

"It's not? Why—did that male do something?" he ground out.

"No. No, it's just my father had little cash flow and…Vincent, what are you doing here?"

Vincent frowned, then smiled.

He really was the most confusing male she had ever met. Why was he smiling at her obvious misfortune? Between the sherry, being manhandled, and the surprise royal visit, Kate's head was spinning. She went to stand, and Vincent lifted her to her feet. Kate brushed her skirts down and smoothed them.

"You look pretty," Vincent said.

"Thank you," she replied, frowning and walking to the cabinet. She needed to think. He obviously wasn't going to give her an answer, and it was entirely frustrating. "Would you like a drink?"

He shook his head. "No."

"Will you tell me why you are here?" Kate asked again.

Suddenly, he was behind her, taking her shoulders in his hands and turning her. "You are not moving into that male's house."

She stared at him. Waiting. "Why? Answer me."

"I came for you," Vincent told her gently.

Warmth spread through Kate's body, right down to her toes. Something akin to hope started growing in her, but she wouldn't dare. She'd been here before with him, and until she heard the words, she wouldn't let herself dream of something which wasn't real again. Never again.

Unless...

"For me?" she asked quietly.

"Yes, Kate. For you," he said, cupping her face. "It appears I am a stupid king, or so my brother says."

A small smile appeared on her lips.

"And I suspect you feel the same way," he added.

She chewed her bottom lip.

He cupped her face. "I was so caught up in not wanting to hurt you or break your heart that I didn't see you were my mate."

Kate's eyes widened.

"From the moment I saw you, I thought you were the most beautiful thing alive, Kate. I was scared to look at you. Scared to touch you. Until I couldn't *not* touch you any longer."

Her lips parted.

Vincent's thumb gently ran over her bottom lip.

"And then, when I held you, when I kissed you, I craved you, Kate," he said a little gruffly. "And still, I was only focused on the pain I could cause you. I couldn't see that you are and have always been the one."

A cry escaped her throat.

"Oh God, Vincent." She felt her legs turn to jelly, but he caught her and held her up against him.

Her chest heaved as she waited. Just a little bit longer for him.

"You are my mate, Kate. Please," Vincent started, moisture in his eyes, "will you be my queen?"

"Oh, God, yes!" she cried as his lips slammed into hers.

Vincent lay with his queen in his arms upstairs in her bedroom. Her eyes were drooping after making love so many times.

It had been the single most incredible moment of his life. All of it. When she said yes. When he saw every inch of her body. When his cock finally slid inside.

And now as she lay tucked into the crook of his arms.

Safe. Protected. Loved

Then he remembered.

As he moved, Kate reached for him sleepily. "Vincent."

"I'm not going anywhere." He smiled.

Ever.

He found his jacket on the floor and dragged it toward him. Reaching in, he pulled out a velvet pouch and climbed across the bed again, wrapping Kate back in his arms. He pulled the ring out and took her finger, slipping it on.

The ring had been his mother's. It had the purest six carat diamond solitaire set in gold.

Kate blinked as he lifted it to his mouth and kissed her hand.

"Queen Moretti," Vincent said. "My most beautiful mate. You have my loyalty, love, and protection until your last breath."

As a tear of joy ran down her cheek, Vincent knew he had been blessed by all the gods.

"You took your damn time, my king."

They smiled.

CHAPTER TWENTY-FOUR

England, 1901

Vincent watched Kate sleep. His queen was a beauty, and over the last ten years, she had won the hearts and minds of the vampire race. She was also the reason they were still living in this damn freezing weather.

He ran his fingers across her forehead, gently moving a lock of hair. She snuggled into him, and his heart roared as it always did. So did his cock, but he attempted to ignore it.

When he'd brought her back to England from Rome, she had convinced him to remain while they sent a team ahead to begin building the castle. A team had been sent to find land and begin construction, and Brayden and Craig had visited to ensure the security was to their liking. Now, the castle was complete, and the royal household could begin their journey.

She had both beauty and brains.

Kate had also wanted to spend time learning and adjusting to being his mate and queen, which was about more than just becoming a member of the royal family. If Kate had been human, Vincent would have drained her blood and replaced it with his own, triggering the change and turning her. That hadn't been necessary, and the two of them had simply bitten each other during a deliciously sexual moment to finalize their bonding.

However, as queen, Kate was required to be infused with the potent Moretti blood.

No one outside the family knew of the secret that their blood held immense power. It made them stronger and helped them heal faster. No one knew exactly how it worked, but after Vincent had received the energy transfer from his father, the old king, he now truly understood the immensity of its power.

So instead of a simple bite and fuck, Vincent had continued drinking from Kate as she drank from him until he'd felt her become stronger and full of the Moretti power. Afterward, Kate had told him she felt amazing.

However, she had shared with him in those early days that she was feeling overwhelmed with all the changes. The loss of her king and queen, losing her own parents tragically, and them finally being together was a lot. And now, her body had changed and been infused with enormous power.

He had no idea what that must be like; he and Brayden had been born with it. So he had felt that loading Kate onto a ship for months and moving her across the world would be selfish.

Once he'd understood, he was happy to stay put. His urgency had only been to escape the agony of not having her. As an immortal, there was never any rush in life.

She flopped onto her back, and he nuzzled into her neck.

One thing that had been a pleasant surprise was how supportive and important his queen had been in helping him become a strong king. He was able to share his concerns, talk through ideas, and listen to hers. Together, they were stronger and so much more.

Thank God for Brayden, or he may have lost her.

"Is it Monday?" she asked, flicking open her eyes gently.

"Yes, my love," he answered excitedly. "Tonight's the night."

The day had finally arrived. They were leaving England and beginning their journey to New York on four ships. With more time, planning, and some thought, they had discovered they needed much more space to move the entire royal household across the seas. They would then make their way up the coast to Maine, where the new Moretti Castle was being built.

Vincent was excited.

The prince was excited.

Their teams were excited.

And now, his queen was excited.

"Well, I'm just going to lie here for a moment longer. I can't imagine the beds on the ships are all that comfortable," she said, turning her back to him.

Vincent laughed and wrapped his body around her. "I had other plans for our last moments in this bed," he whispered, nipping her earlobe as he ran his hand along her smooth, bare bottom.

"I know. I'm just making you work for it." Kate smiled into her pillow.

Vincent lifted her thigh, giving him access to the heat

at her core. He ran his finger through her folds, which were already a little wet. "Am I working hard enough, my queen?"

As he circled his fingers, Kate began to move under him and moan into the plush pillows.

"Mwahgushup."

He raised a brow and smiled to himself, pressing two fingers inside her.

"Goddddd, Vincent," she gasped.

"King will do, baby, just king," he teased, gripping his cock while Kate fought a battle between laughter and pleasure. He needed to be inside her right now.

There was something poignant about their last few hours in England and taking his queen with him. Vincent had overcome his concerns of being a good king with the love of his amazing queen. He was now stronger and more confident with her by his side, and felt he could take on the world.

He pressed his swollen cock inside, holding her hips to go balls deep. "Take me all the way in, baby." Vincent reached to tweak her clit. "I want you dripping wet, baby."

"Yes," she moaned.

Thrusting in and out, he felt her juices surround him. His thumb circled around and around, stimulating her pussy. "More, more, *yes, God*," Kate cried.

Never would he get enough of this female he loved with all that he was. As she fell apart in his arms, he poured into her.

One day, they would produce an heir to the throne. A little piece of both of them to take the vampire race into the future when they were ready to step down. Vincent would make sure there was a different way forward for the Moretti royal family. There was no way he was going to follow in the footsteps of his father and grandfather by losing his head. And fuck, no way would he stand there and let someone take Kate's head. Fuck that.

Vincent intended to create new laws allowing the queen and him to step down and pass on the leadership when their heir was ready. It was a wonderful plan; one Kate was behind. She had been there the day he and Brayden had beheaded their parents at their request.

Yeah, fucked up beyond belief, alright. Nobody wanted to see it happen again.

Except it raised one enormous question: how did he pass on the Moretti power without dying?

The day had finally come. Someone had to solve the eternal mystery behind the source of the power in the Moretti blood, and he had no fucking clue how to do that, given the three of them were the only ones who knew about it.

Weren't they?

CHAPTER TWENTY-FIVE

Present Time

Vincent paced the room as Kate let out another loud cry. God, he wished she'd stop that. Not because he was an unreasonable asshole but because there was no one to blame but himself for the pain she was suffering.

He had done this to her.

He had put this baby inside her.

Yet, he loved this child more than his own breath.

And so the torment continued.

Kate pushed once again.

Push, push, fucking push.

Vincent squeezed her hand. "You've got this, baby. Push."

Fuck you.

"Say that one more time, Vincent Moretti, and I'll push this fucking baby inside you via your asshole."

"That makes zero sense," he said. "Ouch, fuck, those nails. Push again, baby."

"*You* fucking push."

"Okay, you really aren't making any sense. Just do as the midwife says," Vincent instructed her.

Kate threw back her head and let out a really long, loud cry. Mostly because she knew it was driving Vincent crazy and...no, mostly it was that. If she was suffering, he needed to suffer too.

"One more push, Kate," the midwife urged.

For some reason, the female wasn't as irritating as her mate.

The poor vampire had been with them for nearly ten hours. Vincent had called for her despite Kate's assurances, and then the midwife's, that she was hours away from delivering.

In true Vincent style, he'd pointed to a chair and told Vanessa to sit.

"Let's go, one more push," Vanessa encouraged again.

Kate gave it everything she had before collapsing. She was done. The baby could just stay inside her forever. She didn't care.

But then she pushed again, and Vincent leaped to his feet. "Oh my God."

A huge cry let out across the room.

Kate watched as Vanessa handed the baby to Vincent, who stared down at his child, face full of awe and love. She knew that look well.

He glanced at her and placed their child on her chest. "Meet your *mamma*, little one. She's the most incredible female in the entire world."

"Hey, baby," Kate said, brushing her fingers across it's cheek. "Nice to meet you."

"Congratulations, Your Highnesses," Vanessa said before creeping out of the room.

Vincent sat at the head of the bed and wrapped his arms around Kate as they both stared like idiots at their child. They both ran their fingers over every little inch of its body, gently touching its nose and tuft of dark hair, playing with its feet and tiny fingers. Poking at its little mouth.

As if he were the most miraculous thing ever made. And to them, he was.

"He has your hair."

"He does," Vincent agreed, his voice thick. "But your eyes."

"Yeah," Kate said. "He's the most beautiful thing I've ever seen in my life."

"He truly is," Vincent replied. "We made this little vampire."

Kate let out a small laugh. "We did."

"Made with love," he added, grinning. Vincent felt like the gushiest father on the planet, and fuck yeah, he would wear that stupid baby scarf. In fact, he couldn't wait to carry his son around and show him off to the entire world.

"Welcome to the world, Prince Lucas Vincent Moretti," Kate said.

"One day, Lucas, you are going to be a king," Vincent told him, kissing his son on the nose. "Like my father, I am going to teach you everything I know. But I promise you, son, I am going to be by your side as you take the reins. I don't know how I'm going to do it, but I swear I will."

"Vincent. You don't know if you can make that promise," Kate reproached quietly, placing a hand on his cheek.

"I will, Kate. I promise I will."

She smiled at him, a sparkle in her eye.

Neither of them wanted to leave this world. They wanted to meet their grandbaby vamps and watch their family grow as neither of his ancestors had. Vincent wanted a big Moretti family full of Christmas nonsense and annoying reindeer.

"Now, let's get the rest of the family in here to meet you, Prince Lucas."

"Ho, ho, ho." Kate grinned, and tweaked Lucas's nose.

Want to keep reading the Moretti Blood Brothers series? Turn the page to read the first chapter of *The Vampire Assassin*; Ben and Anna's steamy fated-mates love story.

Available February 2022 in paperback or eBook from your favorite online bookstore. Preorder your copy today!

THE VAMPIRE ASSASSIN

CHAPTER ONE

Ben kicked off the white sheet, slammed his large thigh back down on the mattress, and let out a long groan. The apartment he'd rented in Rome was owned by a fellow vampire, so it was well equipped with daytime shutters. It wasn't daylight keeping him awake. It was a female.

Actually, that was a lie. It was his cock.

Every time he closed his eyes…

Yet another lie.

Here's the truth. Ben hadn't been able to stop thinking about Anna since he'd met her yesterday at the Moretti castle while visiting his sister, Sofia De Luca. Which now made it a total of twenty-four hours since he'd been semi-hard, despite jerking off three times already.

Even his hand had had enough.

To make matters worse, Anna had collapsed, so she

hadn't exactly been throwing come-fuck-me eyes at him, although when they'd first spotted each other, the world had slowed down.

In the moment between greeting his sister and taking Anna's hand, he'd learned a lot about the curvy blonde. Which sounded arrogant as fuck, but Ben had been trained to be observant.

Very, very observant.

Kicking off the hard cock campaign were a set of long, thick, dark lashes which had momentarily dropped onto her cheeks in a delicate and submissive manner, doing a little flutter as a warm apricot tinge spread across her heart-shaped face. Her eyes had then lifted, connecting with his, and just before she blinked and began wiping her sweaty palms on jeans which clung to her curves, a sensual glint had given her away.

Those blue eyes had become hooded as he made his way over to her. In those few steps, it was as if Ben lived a million years; he saw Anna with her legs wide, her back arched and head flung back in pure arousal while he clutched her thighs. He felt his thumbs press into her skin as he ordered her not to orgasm until he'd finished with her completely. He tasted her on his tongue as he watched her mouth fall open.

Then, shaking off the vision, he'd taken Anna's hand in his, and it was as if all the pleasure he'd imagined went plowing through their bodies. And he was no fucking poet, but it had struck him like a freight train.

Anna's mouth had parted, and it had taken everything Ben had not to push her to her knees and plant his cock between her red-tinged lips.

Ben kicked off the rest of the sheet and groaned as his hand grabbed his cock.

Yank. At this rate, he was going to yank it right off.

Ben closed his eyes, imagining Anna kneeling before him. He wasn't a dom, but he was an alpha, so a powerful woman in the bedroom didn't excite him as much as a submissive type who opened up her soul and gave herself to him on all levels.

Fuck yes. And he knew if he had a few hours with Anna, that's exactly what she would do.

He needed all that blonde hair wrapped around his fist.

Stroke, stroke.

Cougars—who weren't actually cougars because Ben was over one hundred years old—who took control and rode his cock like wild cowgirls were totally okay with him too. It just wasn't quite as hot.

Tying a willing participant to a post—or any solid object—and adding a few nipple clips to keep the party going when he was busy downstairs got his cock dripping and ready.

Jesus.

His hand gripped harder as he continued to stroke faster, visualizing Anna removing her bra and watching him clip on some of his favorites to her heavy breasts. Her face. He wasn't sure she would've played like this before, and her trepidation and excitement—though imagined—was causing major swelling in the cock area.

His fat crown pulsed as his body shuddered.

He pulled down the zipper on her jeans and slid his hand inside. She'd be wet, her panties soaked…

That was all he needed.

His body jerked, and with a few more tugs, he came all over his thigh. *A-fucking-gain.*

After cleaning up, Ben sat on the edge of the bed and

ran his hand across his face and head a few times.

Shit. What had he done?

Not about wanking off—that he didn't care about.

He'd accepted a job from the king. He started tomorrow.

Ben Ferrero, Lieutenant Commander, in training to step up to be a Senior Lieutenant Commander—or SLC, as they were known. Which was a fucking joke because he *had* a job. Just one he couldn't tell anyone about, especially not the Morettis.

Craig could probe and push all he fucking liked; he'd never get anything out of him, and he wouldn't break. They'd never find out anything about him or The Institute. Or the Director.

Ben grinned.

He'd trained and worked at The Institute for seventy years. There was no way he was going to tell them anything. The great oaf could try all he liked; he'd just grin at the guy. He knew how much Craig loved his dimples.

Was he playing with fire?

Yes.

Did he enjoy it?

Well…maybe. Okay, yes. But life had been pretty damn serious recently. It was only because Sofia had been in trouble that Ben had shown his face. If he'd known she was mated to Lance De Luca—one of the SLCs—he would've kept his distance. It had happened very recently; otherwise, his intel would have been up to date.

Still, once he'd seen his sister after seventy years apart, he had wanted to see her more, at least while he was in Rome on this assignment. Which was how he'd met Anna. He was visiting Sofia at the Moretti castle, and she'd been with the female.

Why? He didn't know. Not history fucking lessons, as she'd tried to tell him.

Little minx.

He intended to find out, before or after he fucked her.

Ben was sure it had something to do with Anna collapsing when Craig and the other warriors had confronted him in the foyer. The stress had set her off, and she'd fallen to the floor shaking. Ben had raced across the room like a mother bear, ready to kill anyone who came near her.

Yeah, that had been weird.

All the males had stayed back, which had surprised him.

Anna had reacted to his voice, calming down, before the king ordered Sofia to take her away. But not before he'd had a quick moment to make her a promise, which he fully intended to keep.

Ben ran his hand over his mouth.

The feeling of Anna's hips under his hands as he whispered into her hair was haunting and delicious.

God, he needed to touch her again.

The king's offer had been a shock both to him and the commander, who, while he hadn't turned purple, had reminded Ben of the Grimace from McDonalds.

Okay, so maybe this could be a bit of fun while he completed his real mission.

The guy needed some healthy competition, and Ben was just the guy for the job. Time to bring the guy down a peg or two.

Ben laughed and climbed back under the sheets.

He'd play along while he found a way to reach Anna again…and eliminated the pending risk to the vampire race; one he knew the king was not aware of, and hopefully, would never need to know about. It was because of the work The Institute did, and its owner, whose identity could not be revealed.

Ari Moretti.

The Vampire Assassin **is available February 2022 from your favorite online bookstore. Preorder your copy today!**

NEW TO THE MORETTI BLOOD BROTHERS SERIES?

Visit your favorite bookstore or: www.juliettebanks.com to keep reading the Moretti Blood Brothers series.

Or join my readers group on Facebook to talk about these sexy vampires.

www.facebook.com/groups/authorjuliettebanksreaders

Printed in Great Britain
by Amazon